D0596663

*A
Harlequin
Romance*

WELCOME
TO THE WONDERFUL WORLD
of Harlequin Romances!

Interesting, informative and entertaining,
each Harlequin Romance portrays an appealing
love story. Harlequin Romances take you
to faraway places — places with real people
facing real love situations — and
you become part of their story.

As publishers of Harlequin Romances, we're extremely
proud of our books (we've been publishing
them since 1954). We're proud also that Harlequin
Romances are North America's most-read
paperback romances.

Eight new titles are released every month and are
sold at nearly all book-selling stores across
Canada and the United States.

A free catalogue listing all available Harlequin Romances
can be yours by writing to the

HARLEQUIN READER SERVICE,
M P.O Box 707, Niagara Falls, N.Y. 14302.
Canadian address: Stratford, Ontario, Canada.

or use order coupon at back of book.

We sincerely hope you enjoy reading
this Harlequin Romance.

Yours truly,

THE PUBLISHERS
Harlequin Romances

THE STORM WITHIN

by

SUE PETERS

HARLEQUIN BOOKS   TORONTO
WINNIPEG

Original hard cover edition published in 1974
by Mills & Boon Limited.

© Sue Peters 1974

SBN 373-01850-9

Harlequin edition published February 1975

The Harlequin trade mark, consisting of the word
HARLEQUIN and the portrayal of a Harlequin, is registered
in the United States Patent Office and in the Canada Trade
Marks Office.

Printed in Canada

1850

CHAPTER ONE

ROB changed gear for the umpteenth time, and regarded yet another twist in the narrow lane with a sigh
of resignation. The heavy foliage of early summer
met overhead on the high banks, and turned the ribbon
of road in front of her into a green tunnel, speckled
with moving splashes of gold where the sun managed
to penetrate the gaps made now and then by the
light breeze.

She manoeuvred the Austin cautiously through the
semi-light, her eyes and ears alert as she nosed the
little car round the U-corner, her right toe gentling
the accelerator pedal, and nerved for instant transfer
to the brake. But nothing appeared in the lane on the
other side of the U, and Hoppy's bonnet rose with a
rattle of protest to meet the steep ascent that seemed
as much a part of the Barshire lanes as those of Rob's
native Devon. Hoppy did not like those, either.

"Sorry, old girl," apologised Rob ruefully, "it's as
bad as being at home!"

But Hoppy ignored her. It had been a long day's
journey from Devon, and her ancient components
were tired.

A T-junction loomed ahead, and the car steamed
to a halt at the white line. Rob thrust her head through
the open window, and surveyed what she could see

of a sagging signpost that leaned precariously against a fence for support. She could not see the writing on the arms for leaves.

"Like everything else in these lanes," she thought in exasperation, "it's smothered in foliage." She had travelled about forty miles through Barshire since she crossed the county line, and had only caught glimpses of it now and then through infrequent gaps in the greenery. The lanes were deep, and the hedges high. "You need a helicopter to see the views in this county," she grumbled disgustedly. "Oh, well, we can only go one of two ways. I'd better find out which."

She twisted the door handle, and applied her shoulder to the door with the ease of long practice. It always stuck. This time it didn't. The door opened with an unprecedented ease that could only have been retaliation, and deposited Rob in an undignified heap, upside down in the middle of the lane.

"Hoppy! You...."

"That is not the way to speak to an old lady!"

Two sturdily booted feet appeared in her range of vision, and a pair of hands reached down and took her arms in a massive grip. The hands were large and sinewy, with a fluff of hairs across the backs that looked oddly pale against the dark, outdoor tan, and contrasted with a work-stained white shirt tucked carelessly into the ample waistband of a pair of faded blue overall trousers. Their grip tightened, and Rob found herself lifted as easily as if she were a child, and gently stood the right way up.

"Do you usually get out of your car in that manner, or is today special?"

The deep voice held laughter, its rich Barshire dialect modified by education to a more understandable speech from that she had encountered when she had lunch a couple of hours ago at a small hostelry along the road. There, she had been barely able to understand mine host, though fortunately he had been able to understand her well enough to produce a satisfying meal.

She screwed up her eyes against the glare of the sun, and squinted at the face above her. It was the same weathered colour as the hands that still gripped her arms, their steely strength belying the fifty-odd years that were betrayed by the lines about the blue eyes regarding her. Her eyes lifted further still, taking in a pair of flaxen eyebrows, and a thatch of hair of the same albino colouring, thinning noticeably at the front.

"It's like icing on the top of a dark fruit cake," she thought irreverently. "At least no one will ever know when his hair turns white."

"Do you think you'll know me again?"

The grin on the man's face broadened, and the lines about his eyes crinkled until his face presented the appearance of a friendly prune. Rob realised with horror that she had been staring at him for fully a minute. A hot tide of colour flushed her normally pale skin, the transparent pallor of the truly auburn-haired, and her lovely amber eyes darkened with embarrassment.

7

"Oh, my goodness! I'm sorry. I mean...oh dear...."

Her voice trailed off, and she put her hands up to her cheeks, an unconsciously childish defence that softened the twinkle in the blue eyes looking down at her. Her own gazed back, wide with dismay, and the man's grin warmed to a smile.

"Don't look so bothered," he chuckled. "Everyone reacts like that at first. I've got a daughter who looks like it, too, only of course she's better to look at than I am," he quipped, talking quickly to cover her embarrassment. "It's our Danish ancestors."

"You don't sound like a Dane?"

"Oh, I'm not. The Wades are as English as Barshire. We come from Wade Hollow, the farm in the dip over there."

He released her, and flung a careless arm towards the corner by the sagging signpost. Rob stood on tiptoe, and followed the direction of his pointing finger, but all she could see was the all-pervading foliage.

"I don't suppose you can see over the rise. You need to be a bit taller to see over Barshire hedges in the summer." The man eyed her trim, trouser-suited figure appreciatively. The soft, amber-coloured jersey wool matched her eyes to perfection, and the cream silk sweater underneath set off the creamy pallor of her face. Her fine skin needed no make-up, and except for a patch of red on one cheek, her short curly hair supplied all her colour.

A frown of concern creased his forehead.

"You're hurt," he declared bluntly. "There's blood on your face."

"There can't be," denied Rob. "My face didn't hit the road."

"No, but your hands did, and you put those to your face just now. Here, let me look."

Disregarding her protest, he took both of her hands in his own, and turned them palm upwards. They lay there, tiny but capable-looking, in his work roughened ones, and he gently straightened the fingers.

"I thought so—gravel rash. Wait here while I get something to wash them with."

He seemed to assume that she would obey him, for he turned his back on her and crossed the narrow lane, disappearing under a stray branch of elderberry, dipping with its weight of bloom, through a field gate that had been previously hidden from her view until the branch swayed away at the behest of the farmer's arm. He reappeared almost at once, with a water container dangling from one hand.

"I've been haymaking in the field on the other side of the hedge," he explained. "I was just going to sit down for a snack when I heard you clank up the hill."

"That was my car clanking, not me," retorted Rob. "We've come a long way today," she explained, somewhat wearily, "and Hoppy doesn't like hills. Or me, at the moment," she added ruefully.

"So it seems," laughed Mr Wade cheerfully. "Here, come and sit on the bank by the gate, and wash your hands with this."

"I don't think it's much," she protested. But her

hands, particularly the right one, were beginning to smart, and as she opened her fingers her right palm oozed blood.

"You can't be too careful." He helped her up the bank, and unscrewed the container cap. "We mustn't have stray travellers getting tetanus. It would give Martyr's Green a bad name."

"Martyr's Green? Why, that's where I'm making for—ouch!"

The water stung as it hit her palms, but the cool of it was soothing, and she held them there, grateful for the steady stream that her companion poured carefully across the grazes until he was satisfied that they were clean.

"I didn't realise I was so close to the end of my trip. To Martyr's Green, I mean."

"You're in it, or at least within the parish boundary," seeing her puzzled look. "The village itself is just past Wade Hollow, about a mile further on, but you. . . ."

"I know. You can't see it for the leaves," chanted Rob, drying her hands on her handkerchief. "I wonder how anyone ever managed to make a map of this county. I've been running through it now for the past two hours, and haven't managed a decent view yet. It's all foliage—and hard lanes," she added ruefully, eyeing her scraped palms.

"Ah, you have to take to the footpaths and walk over the rises to see the views. Rises is Barshire for hills," he explained. "Then you'll see something worthwhile," he added, with all a native's pride. "It's fine farmland around here."

"You said you farmed in the hollow." Rob felt that she ought to be polite, after all, she had used up nearly all of her companion's drinking water to bathe her hands, but the tiredness of the long day's drive from Devon was starting to tell, and she felt herself beginning to flag.

"Yes, if you stand up and look over the gate you can see the chimneys of Wade Hollow among the trees."

He ducked under the elderberry branch, and Rob followed him reluctantly, impatient to be on her way. She longed for a cup of tea, and any other seat but the rather lumpy one that the Austin had to offer.

The farmer came to a halt in front of her, and he moved aside so that she had a space against the gate. It was up to her chin, but she could see well enough over the top bar, though it was too high for her to follow his example and lean her arms along.

"There's a view for you," enthused the farmer proudly. "Like it?"

"It's fine," breathed Rob.

It was not just politeness that put the very real enthusiasm into her voice. The view was indeed lovely, and country bred herself as she was, her heart warmed to the rich green sweep of land falling gently away at their feet to a tree-sheltered hollow several fields distant. And what fields! One of these would easily take four or five of the little red-earthed squares from her native county. Red and white Hereford cattle spotted the intervening green, and Rob's sharp eyes caught sight of the curly forehead of a huge bull.

"There's no footpath through that field, then?" She pointed.

"No." The man regarded her consideringly for a moment, accepting the implications of a rural background from her comment. "It's not against the county laws in Barshire to keep a bull in a footpath field," he added slowly, "but it is against the laws of common sense."

She nodded, appreciating his point, her eyes busy searching the varied green until they picked out the tops of several tall chimneys rising out of a fringe of dark woodland. They gave the impression of a sturdy house underneath, built strong to carry them. A house like that would be safe, she thought, sheltered by the woods.

"Wade Hollow," she murmured. "It's a long way from Denmark," glancing up at her companion's unusual colouring.

"Oh, it's about four hundred years since the Danish member of the clan." He spoke matter-of-factly, without pride. "Our hair is about the only reminder we've got now. I soon won't have that." He laughed indifferently.

Four hundred years in Wade Hollow. They must be an old family.

"Martyr's Green is an old village?"

"It is. Wade Hollow itself is mentioned in the Domesday Book. The place was originally a feudal castle, then a monastery, then a manor house. Now it has to work for a living as a farm. You must come and see it some time if you're staying in the district long enough," he invited. "My wife and daughter are proud of the old place," he told her, completely ignoring his own obvious affection for his ancient home. "They're always willing to show an interested visitor around."

"I'd love to," accepted Rob. "I shall be around for quite a while, I expect. We might even meet professionally."

"Professionally?" The farmer's colourless eyebrows raised in query. "We're all past school age at Wade Hollow, and in perfect health."

"Oh, I'm not a teacher, or a district nurse," said Rob, laughing. "I'm a vet. Not long qualified," she added, with her usual candour. "I've got a job as assistant to your local vet," she explained.

"To Hallam Rand?" The white eyebrows rose still further. "It seems I misjudged the man." His eyes twinkled. "He's not so quiet as I thought."

Rob's ready colour rose again.

"I came to Martyr's Green to work," she retorted, with some asperity. "Mr Rand needs an assistant, and here I am. Or at least, I'm still a mile or so away."

Her voice betrayed her tiredness, and instantly the farmer straightened up from the gate.

"In ten minutes you'll be sitting down in the Mill House and eating one of Martha Main's scones, and drinking some of her tea," he promised.

"Martha who?"

"Main. Hal's housekeeper."

Wade grasped her arm and helped her down the steep bank. She noticed the 'Hal'. It sounded as if the

13

farmer and her future boss were friends, or at least on familiar terms. As a farmer and the local vet would be, she assumed. They would probably be about the same age.

Her feet slipped slightly on the dry grass, and she hesitated. The bank dipped sharply down to the lane below, and her hands tingled a warning of what another tumble could mean. The farmer reached up matter-of-factly, and before she had time to protest he lifted her up and set her down safely on the gravel beside her car.

Rob realised that she had still not looked at the signpost, but it did not matter now, she knew which way to go. She turned to her companion.

"It was good of you to. . . ."

"Pick you up? My pleasure."

The kindly smile broadened, and a spark of temper showed for a second in Rob's eyes. Then, meeting his, she laughed.

"Thank you, just the same, Mr Wade."

"Don't forget what I said about coming to see Wade Hollow," he reminded her of his invitation. "My wife and Verity just love a new pair of ears to pour the history of the old place into," he laughed.

"I won't," responded Rob enthusiastically. It would be pleasant to have somewhere to go, she thought, and someone she knew in a district where she was otherwise a complete stranger. From the look of the farmer, his daughter would probably be a girl of about her own age. It would be nice to make friends, and a common interest in historical buildings would make a good start.

She slid into the driving seat and pressed the starter. As if ashamed of her previous contrariness, the Austin burst into life at the first push.

"Goodbye. And thank you again."

Rob smiled at her rescuer, and waved her hand. He raised his in reply, and as she turned right into the main lane ahead of her, she caught a glimpse of his white head in the driving mirror as he ducked under the low-slung elderberry branch towards the field gate, and his interrupted snack.

CHAPTER TWO

NO sooner had Rob turned right than the T-junction was lost to sight in another series of hairpin bends.

Hoppy seemed to have benefited from her brief rest; she no longer steamed, and the lane soon began to dip, which made the going easier. About half a mile from the junction, a sign painted on a five-barred gate proclaimed the track that led from it towards a distant clump of trees to be the entrance to Wade Hollow. Rob dared not risk more than a glimpse, which gave her no more information than the view from the top of the hill had done.

Just as she thought the bends would never end, the lane gave one final diabolical twist and opened out, unbelievably, on to a village green, complete with a duckpond.

Across the fair-sized stretch of water, the neat sward made a perfect foil for the grey walls of a squat-towered church, dozing peacefully under the inevitable elms. It was surrounded by a cluster of slightly unreal-looking thatched cottages, and completing the picture an ancient set of stocks still stood, offering a deterrent to any local would-be evildoer.

Rob gazed, entranced. It was a scene more reminiscent of a picture postcard than a real life village, and for a wild moment she rubbed her eyes and wondered if it was the effect of tiredness. But when she opened them again the village was still there, placidly asleep under the bright sunshine.

The village pub, thatched as were the other buildings, stood a little aloof, as if shunned by the church and the cottages; its painted sign named it as the Martyr's Arms.

"I bet it's the sort of place where you crack your head on the beams when you stand up," thought Rob. "What a subject for a photograph. Why, there are even ducks on the pond."

She felt glad that she had brought her camera with her. She would send some photographs back to her parents at the first opportunity, she promised herself. They shared her love of old places; it would be fun to rout out the history of Martyr's Green and send it on to them, complete with pictures. It would give a point to her free time until she got to know more people, and add a bit of interest to her letters home.

Home . . .

It suddenly seemed a long way away, and an un-accustomed lump stopped Rob's throat.

"Silly!" she chided herself. "It isn't as if you've never been away from home before."

She thought of her period at veterinary college. Years of study, and hard, grinding work, and then the thrill of qualifying. Her parents had been so proud.

Since then she had spent the intervening six months helping out in the surgery of the local vet. He was a friend of her father, and was willing to let her work under his eye until she obtained a post to suit her. It was an ideal set-up from Rob's point of view, giving her the time she needed to look around. A city practice did not appeal to her. She was used to the freedom of the countryside, views unrestricted by bricks and mortar, and winds that blew clean, untainted by industrial smoke and grime. She did not consider it any sacrifice to turn her back on the life that a town practice might offer, and which had seemed so important to many of the students with whom she had worked.

Hallam Rand's advertisement had caught her eye almost by chance.

"Assistant required for established country veterinary practice. Some experience desirable, but not essential." The address was given as Mill House, Martyr's Green, Barshire.

"Where on earth is Martyr's Green?" asked her mother plaintively, when Rob broached the subject rather carefully at the breakfast table one morning. Her parent's expression suggested that it was at the

17

other end of the world, and did more than suggest that the idea of her daughter forsaking the parental nest, and taking off to places unknown—and so far as she was concerned, unmapped—did not appeal to her.

"I don't know Martyr's Green, but Barshire as a county is pleasant enough," said Rob's father, emerging from behind his morning paper. "Farming county. Mildly hilly." There spoke a Devon man, accustomed to the drastic ups and downs of his native heath. "There wasn't much development there, the last time I drove through. Plenty of space. It's up north, of course, and nowhere near the coast."

North, to her father, started where Somerset ended, and he tried not to sound condemning that Barshire had no coastline. Rob already knew, for she had looked it up on the map, that Barshire was no farther north than the Severn, and the way the advertisement was worded as being a country practice sounded attractive. The word 'country' struck almost a note of warning, she thought, as if the man who put it in had advertised before, and found applicants unwilling to settle in rural surroundings.

So Rob wrote, and to her delight she received back a very pleasant letter from Hallam Rand, offering accommodation at the Mill House, a modest salary, and plenty of hard work, which he disguised tactfully under the description 'varied experience'.

The letter had started 'Dear Rob', which somewhat surprised her, and ended 'Yours sincerely', and the way in which it was couched, in businesslike but friendly terms, made Rob look forward eagerly to her new post.

Her rescuer at the top of the hill had mentioned a housekeeper. A Martha somebody, so the practice must pay well, Rob thought, if his wife could afford to pay a housekeeper. That is, if he had a wife.

"It's funny," she mused, "I don't even know if he is married, or has a family, or anything. Of course, they might be grown-up by now. Maybe he's getting on in years. Perhaps that's why he wanted an assistant. Oh well," she stirred herself out of her reverie, and adjusted her back again to the lumps in the car's front seat, "married or single, young or old, I know for a fact that he's got a housekeeper who serves up fine tea and scones, and I could do with lots of both," she thought hungrily.

She tore her eyes resolutely away from the picture postcard scene on the other side of the windscreen, and slipped Hoppy into gear.

"Come on, old girl. Tea and a tub. I shall feel more human after ... oh, be careful!" she exclaimed aloud.

One of the fat white Aylesburys got up from the pond with unexpected speed, and took off on clumsy wings across her bows. Hurriedly, Rob stamped on the brake. The duck swerved clear, with inches to spare, but a loud crunch from her offside rear wing stated unmistakably that someone else had not been so lucky.

Rob reached for the door handle, and applied her shoulder rather cautiously to the door. It stuck. She braced herself for a heave, but a brown, fine-boned hand forestalled her. Long fingers gripped the door handle, and twisted, and unable to stop herself, Rob hurtled for the second time that afternoon straight through the car door and into the arms of a strange man. Only this time the arms were not friendly. They dumped her unceremoniously on to her feet, and there was no smile in the grey eyes that regarded her with disfavour from nearly a foot above her head. In fact, the scowl that marred the forehead of the thin, ascetic-looking face was almost as black as his hair. One thick wave fell across his forehead, tumbled out of place by the jolt, and he brushed it back impatiently.

"If you must gaze at the scenery, it's safer to do so from your feet than from behind the wheel of a vehicle."

His disparaging glance denied Hoppy even the title of car, and Rob's temper rose.

"I was avoiding one of the ducks," she said coldly. "And anyway. . . ."

"It would have been cheaper for you to have run over the duck, and taken it home for the pot," he interrupted callously, not allowing her to finish her accusation that he had been too close. "You'd better come and see what it's done to your rear wing."

He cupped an imperious hand under her elbow, and without more ado marched her round to the rear of her car. Too surprised to resist, Rob went with him, acutely conscious of the electric tremor of impatience vibrating through the slim, brown fingers curled round her jacket sleeve.

His own vehicle, a sturdy-looking Land Rover, stood behind the Austin, swerved outwards where he had swung his wheel to avoid her. His bumper had caught her rear wing a glancing blow, inflicting an impressive-looking dent.

Rob cast an apprehensive look towards the Land Rover. If it had done that to Hoppy, what on earth must it have done to the chrome on his bumper? She visualised her no-claim bonus receding rapidly.

"It hasn't harmed my vehicle, if that's what you're worried about," commented its owner grimly. "It's built to stand knocks. From the look of it," he added sourly, "your car seems to be accustomed to them," with a pointed look at the Austin's rear mudguard, which showed evidence of hard contact with an un-friendly object—actually, a car which a holidaymaker, unused to the Devon hills, had incautiously left only half braked in the shopping centre of Rob's home town. Hoppy, being the nearest immovable object, parked outside the shops, had stopped the runaway and received a dent in return. That had been last Saturday, and there had been no time to get it repaired before Rob came away.

"That wasn't my fault," she retorted angrily.

"It never is, with a woman driver," returned the dark-haired stranger, with the flicker of a smile in his eyes that Rob was by now too angry to notice.

"It wasn't. . . ."

"Oh, come! I don't care whose fault it was." His grey eyes glinted. "I have to get away." He glanced at his watch impatiently. "Have a look to see if that dent fouls your wheel, in case you need garage help."

He jack-knifed his slender form down beside the

rear wing, without waiting for Rob to answer, and swiftly, her eyes flashing, she knelt beside him.

"I can manage for myself."

"No, you can't. The steel touches the tyre, here. It will rub it bald within a mile if it isn't bent back out of the way. I'll see if I can spring it back for you." He grasped the wing with both hands, probing underneath with long fingers, his eyes remote as he concentrated on his task.

Rob watched him silently, her anger evaporating at his obvious concern to get her on the road again. "Though he probably only wants to get rid of me," she thought ruefully, feeling again the impatience generated by the fingers round her arm.

She hazarded a guess at his profession. A musician, perhaps. Or maybe a doctor. No, not a musician. He did not look old enough, and his neat black head did not look the part. Rob's conception of a professional musician included flowing grey locks. This man did not look a day over twenty-eight. He was probably the local doctor. His hands were those of a professional man, slender, and well cared for. The hands in question moved swiftly on to the edge of the wing, and gave a sharp tug. For a second the steel resisted, then with a clank it unbent itself and sprang back into place with a suddenness that caught the man unawares and trapped his fingers between the over-rider and the edge of the steel.

"Blast!"

Sharply he pulled his hand away, and Rob stood up, quick concern in her eyes.

"You've cut your finger...."

"It's only a graze," he returned curtly, his lips a straight line of barely controlled impatience. "Your car should be movable now, and for heaven's sake exercise a little more care!"

Abruptly he swung himself up into the driving seat of his Land Rover, and with a curt nod started the engine into life, backed off the Austin's bumper, and with an expert swing of the wheel judged his distance to a nicety, rounded the obstruction that was Hoppy, and drove swiftly away.

"Of all the boorish, bad-mannered...."

"Having trouble, miss?"

Rob turned to see a large individual strolling towards her via the edge of the duckpond. His round, brick-red face was topped by a policeman's helmet, made comfortably informal by his jacketless state, and a pair of neat, rolled-up shirt sleeves surmounting muscular arms more befitting of a smith than a policeman.

When she was driving, Rob's normal reaction on being confronted by the law was to feel guilty, whether she had infringed the parking regulations or not, but she warmed at once to his cheery approach, so different from the stormy encounter that was just over.

"Not really. More of a misunderstanding," she smiled back.

"I thought as much. That's why I kept inside." He waved to one of the thatched cottages, with the regulation 'Police' notice shakily tacked to the bulging wall.

"Actually, I'm on my way to Mill House. Now

you're here, perhaps you can direct me?" asked Rob hopefully.

"The vet's place?"

"That's right. I'm going to work for the vet, as his assistant," she explained. If this was the village policeman, he would soon get to know who she was anyway, and as he seemed inclined to be friendly Rob thought she might as well meet him half way. She had every motorist's urgent desire to remain friendly with the law.

"Well, I'm blessed! You haven't started off very well, have you?" said the policeman sympathetically.

"By getting my car bumped, you mean? Oh well, not everyone can be as bad-tempered as the Land Rover driver was," smiled Rob optimistically.

"Eh? Oh, I see what you mean." An odd look of caution came over his rubicund face, and he eyed Rob strangely. "So you're going to work for the vet, at Mill House? You do mean Hallam Rand, I take it?"

"Yes, that's right," nodded Rob. "He needs an extra pair of hands in the practice, it seems, and I'm here to supply them."

"He needs that, all right," confirmed the policeman. "There's a lot of work in a farming community like this, and he's the only vet between here and Barhill. That's our market town, and it's twelve miles away," he added thankfully.

"I'll find my way there one day soon," said Rob, "but in the meantime, I've got to find Mill House," she hinted.

"Oh yes, of course. Well, you can't miss it," her

companion said, with the classic assurance of a local who knows every inch of the ground. "Go along the main street here, over the river bridge, then turn sharp right along the course of the river. You'll see Mill House on the bank."

"It really is a mill, then? I didn't know you had a river so close?"

"Oh yes, the Bar is a fair-sized stretch of water. Good for trout." So the village policeman was also a fishing enthusiast. "You must have come in from the other side of the village. You wouldn't see it from there."

"Because of the trees, I expect," laughed Rob, familiar by now with at least one local drawback.

"That's right." The policeman did not seem to see anything amusing about the foliage, and Rob straightened her face dutifully. "It runs from the other side of the village, through the land at Norton End Farm —that's the holding at the back of the Martyr's Arms here—and cuts across the side of the village. As I said, you can't miss Mill House."

Hoping fervently that he was not being literal, Rob thanked him and resumed her seat in the car. Soon she came to the bridge over the Bar. As the policeman had said, it was a good-sized stream, and looked deep. She turned right as he directed, and a couple of hundred yards in front she saw the stark outlines of a millwheel, black against the sky, lazily throwing up bright drops that sparkled in the sunshine as it turned at the behest of the current underneath.

With a sigh of relief Rob switched off the engine

and relaxed, tiredness sweeping over her in a wave now that the day's drive was done. The Mill House looked old, and its warm-coloured walls invitingly friendly, squatting low beside the water. She reached for her case and mounted the two shallow steps to the studded door. The bell was of the old-fashioned, rope-pull kind, and it gave an unexpectedly harsh clang which brought an immediate response from inside.

The woman who confronted her across the step was amply proportioned, and elderly. "Comfortable," thought Rob, with relief. 'Not one of these smart housekeepers." A pair of bright blue eyes under a silvery knot of hair, scraped back into an old-fashioned bun, regarded Rob with enquiry.

"I'm Rob Fenton," she introduced herself. "I've come to work for Mr Rand. I take it that you're Mrs Main?"

She held out her hand. For a brief second the older woman seemed to hesitate, then she pulled herself together and took Rob's hand rather uncertainly.

"*You're* Rob Fenton?" She eyed Rob's slight figure with a look of disbelief in her eyes that puzzled the girl. The housekeeper did not seem unfriendly, but she certainly looked taken aback.

"Perhaps she doesn't approve of trouser suits," thought Rob, and wished that she had travelled down in a dress instead.

"Well, come in, my dear, come in. What am I doing, keeping you here at the door like this?" The housekeeper looked flustered.

"I wrote to say I was coming today. Did Mr Rand

not get my letter?" asked Rob. She had given it to her father to post, and if he had left it in his jacket pocket. . . .

"Oh yes, he got your letter. Everything is ready for you, but. . . Oh well, you must be tired after your long journey. Come away in, and have a cup of tea. Dinner won't be for another hour, depending on when Mr Rand gets in."

"Is he out on a call?"

"Yes, he's had to go out to a cow that's having difficulty in calving. He'll be back in time for dinner, though, I imagine. He usually is."

The housekeeper led the way through a cool, panelled hall, bright with flowers. The heady scent of roses wafted through an open window, and Rob caught a glimpse of colourful borders lining a smooth lawn, and the glitter of water beyond. There was little sound in here from the river, only an occasional rumbling noise that she assumed came from the mill wheel.

"Come up to your room and get rid of your case, then when you've had time to freshen up you can put your car away."

"Oh yes, please. Hoppy will be as glad of a rest as I shall."

"Hoppy, is it? Well, I hope she behaved on the journey here." The elderly woman led the way up a wide staircase, and opened the door of a room leading from the landing at the top. "I've put you in here. If there's anything you want, just call me. You'll see where the garage is, at the back, from your window. Then when you're ready I'll set you some tea in the study, unless you would like to come into the kitchen and have yours with me? I'd just put the kettle on when you rang."

"Oh yes, please. I would much rather." Rob warmed to the kindly smile and the soft, Barshire voice. "I'll be with you in a few minutes."

She crossed to the wash basin, and splashed water over her hot face. It was beautifully soft, and she reached for the soap, a little surprised to find it was plain carbolic. Perhaps they were old-fashioned, but she did not mind that; she could always buy some of her favourite toilet soap later on. Her room looked comfortable, anyway. It was very plainly furnished, but an experimental bounce on the bed confirmed that it was soft, and the windows looked straight out on to the river. The quiet murmur of the wheel filled the room, and she smiled. If the job was going to be as pleasant as the living quarters, she would enjoy her stay at Mill House.

She berthed Hoppy in an ample little shed at the back of the house, left open for her by Martha Main, and sought the housekeeper in her kitchen. A yeasty smell of baking guided her to the right door, and Martha's bright smile welcomed her in. She pulled out a chair and sat down at the scrubbed table, happily adorned with a large plate of buttered scones, hot from the oven, and an equally large pot of tea.

"If you would rather have yours in the study, Miss Fenton?"

"Oh no, it's much nicer having it in here with you," smiled Rob, "and please call me Rob. It will be friendlier now that I'm to work here."

The smile on the other's face widened.

"And you must call me Martha. But. . . ." Again the hesitation, and the puzzled look.

"But what?" Rob smiled encouragingly.

"Well, I don't want to seem rude, but isn't yours rather an unusual name for a girl?" said the other hesitantly.

"Oh, that. It's Roberta, really," explained Rob. "When my parents knew that I was on the way, they prepared for a boy. When I arrived, they had to think again. They'd chosen Robert, so they just added an 'a'," she mumbled, her mouth full of scone. "These are delicious, Martha. I was so hungry." She sighed contentedly.

"Have another one, do."

"Not another crumb, or I shan't have enough room for dinner." But she accepted a second cup of tea, and sipped it happily.

A car door slammed just outside the house, and Martha got up from her chair. "That sounds like Mr Rand."

She disappeared through the kitchen door into the hall, and Rob heard a man's voice.

"I'm afraid I'm a bit late, Martha, but I'd love a cup of tea if you've got your usual brewed."

"Is the cow all right, Mr Hal?"

"The cow is doing fine, but it was no thanks to me." The deep voice sounded grim. "I got there later than I intended. A fool woman motorist stopped without warning, right in front of me on the village green, and

I had no chance to avoid her. By the time I'd straightened out her apology for a car, it delayed me at least a quarter of an hour."

"Oh no! It can't be. . . ." Rob's hands hovered over her ears, sheer disbelief urging her to shut out the hateful sound of his voice.

Martha appeared at the door, and behind her the tall, dark-haired figure of her acquaintance from the village green.

"I'll have my tea in here with you, Martha. I can't stay for more than a few minutes. I must go back again, to make sure the cow. . . . Good heavens! Whatever brings you here?"

He stopped dead in the doorway, and stared at Rob with irritation written all over his face. Martha turned to him.

"This is Miss Fenton, Mr Hal. *Miss Rob* Fenton," she emphasised, and even through her dismay Rob felt again the odd tone of voice in which Martha emphasised her name.

CHAPTER THREE

"THERE'S no need for him to look at me like that," thought Rob angrily, temper conquering her dismay. "I haven't wrecked his beastly Land Rover. Anyone would think I ran into him, instead of him running into me!"

Certainly, the housekeeper's feelings seemed to be duplicated in Hallam Rand. Consternation was written all over his face. If a minor bump could cause him to look like that, what on earth would a major accident do? wondered Rob crossly. Suddenly her patience snapped. She was tired from her journey, and had the beginnings of a headache which even the tea and scones had done nothing to alleviate, and if this was the effect she had on her new employer, then they might as well call off the arrangement now, and she would go back to Devon and continue her work there. Obviously, her appointment with this man would never work out.

She stood up swiftly, the ready colour staining her cheeks.

"I apologise if I delayed you on a call," she said stiffly, "but it was your own fault for driving too close behind me. I had to make an emergency stop, and if you'd obeyed a few commonsense rules of the road, you wouldn't have careered into me as you did. If you don't believe me, take a look at the Highway Code," she flashed angrily. "Now, if you'll excuse me, I'll collect my belongings from upstairs, and leave. I expect I can get a room at the inn in the village for the night."

She moved towards the door impulsively, but stopped nonplussed when the man stood his ground, and made no move to let her through. He remained where he was, leaning casually on the door jamb, his other hand on the knob of the half-opened door, effectively blocking her exit. Rob noticed guiltily that he had a bandage on his finger. The bemused look was still on his face, but a faint gleam of humour, or it could have been admiration, flared for a moment in his eyes, but once again Rob was too angry to notice.

After what seemed a long time he straightened his lithe body away from the jamb, though he still kept his hand on the knob, making it impossible for her to go through.

"I stand corrected, Miss Fenton." His voice held an undercurrent of amusement, which did nothing to calm Rob's annoyance. "I was much too close behind you," he admitted.

Rob stared at him, taken aback by his volte-face.

"Then what's bothering you ...?" she began, for disconcertment still lay heavy over both the vet and his housekeeper.

"You are," retorted Hallam Rand bluntly, the laughter vanished from his voice. "When you wrote to me, if you remember you simply signed your letter 'Rob Fenton'. I took it to be short for Robert," he said simply. "When I engaged you as my assistant, I thought that I was employing a man."

So that was why they both looked at her as if she came from another planet! Enlightenment dawned on Rob, and with it came an urgent desire to laugh. Sternly she suppressed the inclination. In the face of the two troubled countenances regarding her across the kitchen, it would not be seemly to give way to merriment, and she wanted this job at Martyr's Green more than ever. She had fallen in love with the village, and wanted to explore it, and the surrounding countryside, as well as take up the invitation she had had to see over that farm. 'Something-or-other Hollow,' the farmer had called it. She supposed in a way that it was her own fault that the misunderstanding had arisen. She had signed her name to the letter, under-lined it with a flourish and crossed fingers, and never given a thought to the consequences of not adding 'Miss'. That accounted for the odd reception that she had received from the housekeeper, and the spartan cake of soap in her room.

Deliberately, Hallam Rand closed the kitchen door, removed his hand from the knob, and cupped it under Rob's elbow.

"Sit down again for a moment, Miss Fenton. This situation is as difficult for you as it is for me."

With his free hand he pulled out a chair for her, and Rob took it automatically. She did not see where any difficulty lay, but she reacted to his friendlier tone, and waited quietly for him to go on. Martha looked relieved, and hastily filled two more cups. Rand took his, and stirred it slowly, as if he was gathering his thoughts.

"When you answered my letter, you said you were satisfied with my qualifications," prompted Rob.

"Oh yes, there's no difficulty there. You seem to have acquitted yourself very creditably at college. And the reference you enclosed from your local vet was more than satisfactory." He sounded quite enthusiastic.

"I'm strong enough for a country practice," Rob assured him hastily. She could not very well flex her muscles and show him, but she sat up straighter in her

33

chair, and hoped that it made her look taller than she was. "I told you I'd been with a country vet for the last six months, and I took the rough with the smooth, along with him." She did not want to confine her work to the poodle and budgerigar brigade of some bricks-and-mortar suburb, however lucrative the living might be.

"I don't doubt your—er—ability." Again his voice held that faint undertone of amusement, and his grey eyes regarded her stiffly held figure with something suspiciously like a twinkle.

"Then I don't see why. . . ." began Rob.

"Surely you must see that it's an unsuitable arrangement," retorted the vet, exasperation chasing the amusement from his eyes. "It's not only the job, it's the accommodation. . . ." He shot a rather helpless glance at his housekeeper.

"Miss Fenton will be quite all right here with me, Mr Hal," said Martha. "There's no difficulty that need stand in your way there. None at all," she emphasised firmly.

Rand looked at her, uncertainty beginning to chase the resolve from his thin—too thin—face.

"You need the help, Mr Hal, you know you do." Martha pushed her point. "You simply can't go on day after day doing the work of two men, as you are now. Why not give it a trial for a month?" she coaxed. "After all, if it doesn't work out, for either you or Miss Fenton, you can always part company at the end of that time," she insisted. "It would be help for you, that you know you badly need, and experience for Miss Fenton."

"Rob," insisted Rob.

"Miss Rob, then," Martha smiled at her. "At least give the lass a trial, after the journey she's had to get here." Martha made it sound as if Rob had started from the North Pole that morning.

Rob began to feel uncomfortable under the vet's hesitation. She did not want to hold any job on sufferance, not even this one, that she decided with a characteristic streak of stubbornness she now wanted more than any other job in the world.

"If my being here is going to cause difficulties ..." she began stiffly, but Martha silenced her with a decided shake of her grey head.

"None that matter," she countered. "Now, drink your tea, Mr Hal, so I can clear up and start preparing the dinner."

The vet emptied his cup and put it down on the table, still regarding Rob with more than a hint of vexation on his face. Clearly, he did not think very highly of women who signed abbreviated names, and thereby placed him in this sort of predicament. Though what his predicament was, Rob was still not clear.

He got up and pushed his chair back.

"I must go back and have another look at that cow," he said, and his voice sounded suddenly weary. He glanced down at Rob. "It might be best to do as Martha says," he said reluctantly, his voice betraying his complete lack of enthusiasm for the idea. "Are you agreeable to remaining for a month on trial, with the probability of having to obtain another job at the end of it?"

"Quite agreeable," replied Rob crisply. He had said 'probability', not 'possibility', so as far as he was concerned, the outcome was already decided. "We can see how things work out," she told him, her voice devoid of expression, "and then discuss it in a month's time."

"Very well." His manner reverted to the aloof constraint of their encounter by the duckpond, and he gave her an impersonal nod. On his way out he glanced at Martha, and his look held an odd kind of appeal. The elderly woman's eyes were soft as they met his.

"On your way, now," she said quietly, "and try not to be late for your dinner."

She spoke affectionately, with more than just the privileged familiarity of an old servant, and Rob sensed a warmth between the two. She reached for a glass cloth as Martha ran water into a bowl. The housekeeper looked surprised, and her ready smile returned.

"There's no need for you to help me with these unless you want to."

But she did not actually tell Rob to leave them alone. She seemed to sense her need for company, and busied herself with the cups without saying anything more until they were dried and stacked. Rob was equally quiet, absorbed in her own thoughts, and not finding them the best of company. It would be a disastrous start to her career if she lost this job, for no other reason than that she was a girl.

Martha clicked the last of the crocks together, and broke the silence.

"You mustn't worry too much about Mr Hal, Miss Rob," she said slowly. "It was a bit of a shock for him, discovering that you were a woman. For me, too," she added with a smile.

"I wondered why you hesitated, when you answered the door," replied Rob. "It's understandable, I suppose, and mostly my own fault. But why make a difficulty of it? Will his wife object, or what?"

"Mr Hal is single." Martha's voice was gentle. "That's where the difficulty lies, in his eyes. He's thinking of you, my dear. He forgets that I make an adequate chaperone, even in the eyes of a small village like this."

"Oh!" Understanding dawned on her, and Rob chuckled. "How old-fashioned! But he needn't worry about me," she assured the housekeeper. "I've come to work as his assistant, not to give the village gossips a heyday. Anyhow, he doesn't even like me very much," she added, her voice unconsciously forlorn. "The village policeman was a witness to our first meeting," she remembered ruefully, "and even he had the good sense to keep out of the way until Mr Rand had gone," she added gratefully.

"Ah, that would be Alf Dodd. He's a sensible soul," remarked Martha, nodding. "But Mr Hal isn't really bad-tempered," she assured Rob, "he's just over-worked. It makes him a bit impatient at times."

'A bit impatient' was hardly the description Rob

would have given to the vet's seething irritation at their first meeting, but she let it pass without comment.

"You won't have to mind if he's a bit reserved," the housekeeper went on, in a confidential tone. "He's not much used to girls."

"Not used to . . . ?" Rob's sense of wonderment increased. In her world, filled with a host of friends of both sexes, and an easy-going ability to mix with them all, such a thing was an alien quality. She said as much to her companion.

"I expect you've been lucky, with a home and a family," said Martha.

Rob nodded.

"Well, Mr Hal has had a very different upbringing." She reached for a bowl of new potatoes and began to scrape busily. "His uncle was a bachelor, and the vet here before him. When Mr Hal's parents died—his father was a soldier—he was sent back from India, and his uncle brought him up."

"No wonder he's wary of women, if he was reared in an all-male household," said Rob, understanding better now.

"Not entirely male. I was here," replied Martha comfortably. "He was but a wee lad then. His uncle was fond enough of him, but he hadn't got much time to spare for a child, running the practice single-handed as he did, and I brought up Mr Hal," she added, her voice revealing her affection as she spoke of her employer.

That explained the closeness that Rob had sensed between the two of them.

"He's very lucky to have you," she said aloud, using the present tense deliberately. Despite her reservations about the vet, she liked the elderly housekeeper, and knew instinctively that her liking was returned. It was not comforting, however, to realise that her job relied on Hallam Rand's good opinion, after their unfortunate first meeting, and now the misunderstanding over her name.

"Oh, I look after him all right. But I'm no company for him," said Martha. "He needs companions of his own age."

"Surely there are some facilities for relaxation, even in Martyr's Green? Dances, and whist drives, and. . . ." Rob drew on her knowledge of the busy social life of her home village. "And if Mr Rand was brought up in the village, he must know the people who were children here at the same time as he was." If the man chose to be a recluse now, he could not always have been so, she thought, feeling exasperated in her turn. "He must have gone to school."

"That was half the trouble. He was sent to boarding school." Martha's tone suggested that it was the equivalent of a prison sentence. "He would have been better off here at the village school, learning to mix with all the other children, boys and girls. As it was, at boarding school he only had boys for company, and it brought him up shy. Of girls, I mean."

Rob would not have described her new employer as shy, either. She deferred to Martha's superior knowledge of the man, but in her limited experience of the vet he had not been shy in expressing his opinion of her driving, nor backward in his caustic remarks about Hoppy. She bit her lip vexedly at the thought of his disparaging summing up of her beloved Austin.

"A lot of adults are shy. They usually manage to cope," was all that she could think to say. She perched on the edge of the table, watching Martha busily slicing the naked potatoes.

"Oh, he manages all right," replied the housekeeper, "and of course he's got Miss Verity, so it doesn't really matter."

"Miss Verity?"

"Verity Wade," explained the elderly woman. "She lives at one of the farms around here, Wade Hollow."

"Oh, I know. The one with the white-haired farmer. He said he had a daughter named Verity," remembered Rob.

"I didn't know that you knew them?" Surprise showed in the housekeeper's face. "I thought you were strange to these parts?"

"So I am. But Mr Wade picked me up on the way here. Literally." Rob showed Martha her grazed hands, and explained.

The housekeeper clucked disapprovingly at the raw marks, and hurried to a white cabinet in the corner.

"You must get those properly washed. Here's something to put on them." She handed Rob a tin of what looked like salve of some sort. "We can't have you getting tetanus."

"That's just what Mr Wade said. But I don't think there's much danger. . . ."

She accepted the tin just the same, and Martha shooed her towards the door.

"Go and see to them right away. You never know. . . ."

"While I'm up there, I might as well unpack," said Rob.

"If you're going up to your room, take this with you." Martha reached into a store-cupboard and brought out a packet of perfumed toilet soap. Their eyes met, and Rob laughed.

"Thanks, I will."

She was still chuckling as she went about putting her clothes in the drawers, and tidying up the inevitable debris of travel. At any rate, she liked Martha, and she did not suppose she would see much of the vet himself, except during their working hours, when they would be too occupied to like or dislike one another, she guessed correctly.

Finished at last, she flicked a brush through her bright curls and slipped into a sleeveless dress of pale green silk, with a pair of green strapped sandals to match. It would do for this evening, she was too tired to make much fuss, though the brief period alone in her room had soothed her headache away. The gentle murmur of the mill wheel had a soporific effect, and she felt too drowsy to care for the moment what the outcome of the next month would be. She realised that she was hungry, and made her way downstairs.

Martha came out of the kitchen door just as she reached it.

"I've laid dinner in the study, Miss Rob," she said, and indicated the door of a room on the other side of the hall.

"Oh, I thought...."

"Naturally you'll take your meals with me."

A calm voice behind her turned Rob round, and Hallam Rand came into the hall through a door that obviously led out on to the garden. He waited for a second, his hand on the knob, and a slender red setter appeared behind him. As soon as the dog was safely through, Rand shut the door and turned to her.

"This way."

His hand rested briefly on her shoulder as he guided her towards the door that Martha had indicated. He held it open for her to go through, then followed with the setter close at his heels.

Rob stopped just inside, and gave an exclamation of pleasure.

"What a lovely room!"

Her eyes took in the pale walls, panelled like the hall, and the comfortable easy-chairs, strewn about a low brick fireplace, filled with flowers now as a concession to the warmth of the day. A bookcase filled one entire corner beside the fire, flanked by a writing desk, and the whole was made cosy by a soft carpet almost the amber of Rob's trouser suit, and velvet curtains of the same rich shade, pulled well back from the big windows. French doors stood open on to a lawn, and a small table, set for two, was pulled to one side of them, the better to take advantage of the slight breeze blowing in, bringing with it a heavy perfume from the well stocked rose borders dotted about the lawn, and another, sweeter scent that Rob recognised as orange blossom, though she could not see where it came from. The view was the same as from her bedroom, and she realised that they were directly below it, though nearer to the mill wheel, which seemed louder in here.

"Does the sound worry you?" enquired Rand, pulling out one of the chairs for her. "We generate our own electricity here, by means of power from the stream," he explained. "It's deep, and has a powerful current, so we always have a plentiful supply of power."

"What a sensible idea. No, I find it soothing."

Rand took his seat opposite to her as if she was an invited guest, rather than an unwelcome surprise in his household. He behaved as if the brush on the village green had never occurred, and Rob relaxed slightly, though still on the defensive. She had, after all, fallen foul of him twice in one short afternoon, and she did not want to risk it a third time. Three might not prove to be lucky. As soon as he had seen to her immediate needs, and made sure that she had everything she wanted, the vet relapsed into silence, his face withdrawn. Rob wondered if anyone would ever get to know him really well. Anyone, that is, except Martha. And, of course, Verity Wade.

The setter turned himself round and round several times, then settled down quietly beside his master.

Hallam Rand looked across his soup bowl at Rob.

"Don't mind Red. He always stays with me. He'll be no bother to you at all," he half apologised for the dog's presence at the meal table.

"Red ignores everyone else's existence except Mr Hal's," smiled Martha, coming in with the vegetables. She served them both deftly and disappeared kitchenwards, and they continued to eat in silence. Beyond necessary politenesses, Hallam Rand offered no conversation, and Rob followed his lead and remained silent. She would have liked to talk, liked to learn a little about the practice, and the village. Even the man himself, since she would be working with him, if it was only for the one month, but she did not care to break the barrier that he seemed to have put up in front of him. He ate with the deliberation and economy of time of one accustomed to solitary meals, taken without minutes to spare. Studying him across the table, Rob wondered if any conversation could reach beyond that remote mask opposite to her. It was a younger face than she had at first thought, but lines that spoke of weariness etched the corners of his eyes. Martha had accused him of doing the work of two men, she remembered, and his looks reflected the truth of what she said.

Rob gave her attention to her dinner, which was excellent. Martha certainly knew how to cook, and Rob complimented her when she came in later with a tray of coffee. The elderly housekeeper beamed.

"You must have been ready for it, dear." She indicated the coffee. "If I put this on the table by the fireplace, will you serve it when you're ready?"

Rob nodded acquiescence, and moved over to a chair near the coffee table.

"How do you like yours, Mr Rand?"

"Black, thank you."

That explained the rather small jug of cream standing on the tray. Rob handed him his darkly filled cup, and he took it from her and reached out towards a pipe rack beside a large armchair against the fireplace. He had a pipe in his hand when suddenly he hesitated, as if remembering her presence.

"Do you mind if I smoke?"

"Not at all," Rob smiled. "My father does, so I'm used to it."

She liberally whitened her own coffee, and curled up in a chair on the opposite side of the fireplace. She assumed the chair by the pipe rack would be his. Her guess justified itself when he sat down, and the setter curled up on the rug beside him, again taking two or three turns before he lay down.

Rob would have preferred to take her coffee with Martha; it would have been friendlier, and the elderly woman would probably have talked to her. She missed the company at home, and the family habit of sharing the news of the day over the evening meal, that made it such a pleasant time to look forward to. With her employer, conversation had been non-existent at dinner, but with eating to occupy them the silence had not been too oppressive. She did not relish spending the rest of the evening in the same atmosphere, tinged, she felt sure, with disapproval—first of her driving, then of her carelessness over the signing of her letter of application.

The man dropped heavily into his chair, and after a couple of abortive attempts eventually got his pipe going to his satisfaction. The sweet smell of good tobacco mingled with the perfume of the flowers, and Rob relaxed against her cushions, drowsy with the effects of good food, and the long day's driving.

She glanced towards her companion, and became conscious of an unwavering stare from the setter's eyes, as amber as her own.

"He's like Ricky," she thought wistfully, remembering the setter she had had as a child. Those carefree days in Devon seemed a world away now. An unconscious sigh escaped her lips, and brought a sharp glance from the man. She looked very young, and very vulnerable, curled in one corner of the big armchair. Dark smudges marked her eyes, and her head dropped back on the cushion in surrender to her long day, warning the vet not to talk shop with her tonight. The big chair dwarfed her slight figure, and the delicate material of her dress clung like softly rounded jade, accentuating the creamy pallor of her arms and throat. She looked at the dog, and smiled. Red responded with a slight wave of his tail. Martha had said that he always ignored anyone else but his master, but she had drawn a definite response from him. Rob liked dogs. She made no move towards the setter, but she smiled again, and this time he got up slowly and padded across to her. Without altering her position she

46

laid her hand, palm upwards, on her knee, her eyes still on those of the dog. For a long moment the setter held her gaze, and then his tail waved, and he dropped his muzzle into her palm.

"Well, I never! That is the first time I've ever seen Red do that to anyone but you, Mr Hal," exclaimed Martha wonderingly. She rested the tray of dinner crocks on her hip, and gazed at the dog with something akin to awe. "You've certainly made a hit there, Miss Rob!"

"It seems to be a habit of hers," commented Hallam Rand drily, and Rob flushed. He need not have brought that up again tonight, she thought crossly, and he had already admitted that he was driving too close to her anyway. She fondled the setter's silky ears gently, not looking at him, afraid that he might see the vexation in her eyes if she did.

"I should have an early night after your drive up, if I were you, Miss Rob," advised Martha, still watching her and Red, and she looked up at the housekeeper gratefully, glad of the excuse to quit the room.

"I think I will. Unless . . . ?" She looked up at Hallam Rand enquiringly.

"Nothing tonight," said the vet. "Get a good night's sleep, and you can start at surgery tomorrow. Goodnight, Miss Fenton," he said gravely.

Thankfully, Rob said good-night, gave the setter's ears another rub, and stood up, glad to make her escape before she either went to sleep in the chair and disgraced herself, or upset her obviously touchy employer once again.

Twice in one day, she felt, was quite enough for a start.

CHAPTER FOUR

THE last sound that Rob heard before she went to sleep was the soft murmur of the mill wheel, and it filled her room when she opened her eyes the next morning, to find the sun playing patterns on the ceiling, and Martha standing by the side of her bed with a cup of tea in her hand.

"Heavens, what's the time? Have I overslept?"

She sat bolt upright, rubbing her eyes.

"No, there's plenty of time, it's only just past seven," said Martha, "but I thought you might like this to start the day. Breakfast won't be for another half hour or so yet."

"Bless you!" Rob accepted the cup and sipped gratefully. Her face was flushed with sleep, and her hair clung in soft curls close to her head. In her plain white nightdress she looked very young.

"What time does Mr Rand start surgery?" she asked, her mind already busy on the day ahead.

"Not until nine o'clock. But you'll have to start it on your own this morning, Miss Rob. Mr Hal was called out to that cow again at six o'clock, and the farmer has just phoned to say he won't be back for at least another couple of hours. They'll give him breakfast over there."

"Where is there?" asked Rob, eager to know the lie of the farms, for they would inevitably provide the bulk of the work in the practice.

"Wade Hollow. You met the farmer yesterday when you fell out of your car."

"They're hospitable at Wade Hollow," commented Rob, referring to Hallam Rand's breakfast.

"Oh, they're old friends of Mr Hal," returned Martha comfortably. "He and Verity were children together. He practically lived at Wade Hollow as a lad."

It sounded as if he still did, and not entirely in his professional capacity, either. She handed Martha her empty cup, and the housekeeper made to go.

"Come down when you're ready," she bade Rob easily, "but give yourself time for a good breakfast. Surgery is usually busy, and you won't have time to think until mid-morning, if then," she warned.

The surgery proved to be as good as Martha's word. The waiting room was full when she opened the door, and by eleven o'clock Rob had dressed so many cut paws, torn ears and bite wounds that she began to believe that every dog and cat in the neighbourhood had joined in one glorious free-for-all.

"It must be the hot weather," grumbled one weary owner resignedly. "It makes them irritable."

The cup of sweet coffee that Martha brought her mid-morning was accepted with alacrity, and instantly given to the weeping owner of an aged cat that Rob had had no recourse but to put to sleep.

"I'll find you a kitten, and bring it along one day

soon," she assured the old lady, putting her into a chair.

"Oh, will you, miss? I'd be that grateful." Her worn face brightened. "I live on my own, you see."

"I'll be over just as soon as I can," promised Rob. "In the meantime, will you see about making up a nice soft bed for the kitten? Oh, and you'll have to think up a name for it as well," she tried to distract her.

"I could call it Ginger, after...."

"But it may be black, we don't know yet," intervened Rob hastily, as tears threatened again. "Now, what about that bed for it?" she hinted.

"I've got some odd wool, I can knit a bit of a blanket." Interest began to sound in the wavering voice.

"That will be splendid," encouraged Rob. "You must show me what you've managed to do when I bring you the kitten."

She patted the old woman's shoulder, and sighed as she shut the door behind her. This was a part of her job that she hated. Martha reappeared with another cup of coffee as she turned back into the surgery.

"Oh, Martha, you shouldn't!"

"Well, I saw where the other one went," said the housekeeper, mock-stern.

"I couldn't help it. She was so upset."

"I'll keep my eyes open for a kitten for you," promised the housekeeper, her face softening. "There must be plenty about at this time of the year. Now drink your coffee while it's hot."

"If you'll give me a cup as well, I'll tell you where to find six kittens, assorted colours, for free," offered a voice from the doorway. "Stay there, Mel. I'll come back for you," it went on, to something or someone out of sight in the waiting room.

"Come along in, Miss Verity," called Martha, recognising the voice. "I'll go and get your coffee for you," she promised. "You've come to see Miss Fenton, I expect," she prophesied, indicating Rob.

"Right in one," smiled the owner of the voice, appearing round the door.

Rob smiled back. She could not help it. The girl's tanned, open face and blue eyes were disarmingly friendly, and her pale, silver-blonde hair, tied carelessly back from her face with a blue ribbon as faded as her jeans, was a replica of her father's, only hers fell in a thick, clubbed mane, heavy to her slender waist. She was strikingly handsome, and seemed quite unconcerned about the fact.

"Hall went on his rounds direct from the Hollow," said Rob's visitor casually, "so I thought I'd drop in and let Martha know—and second my father's invitation to come and see round Wade Hollow," she invited Rob. "I believe you're interested in old buildings. Dad told us he met you yesterday."

Her dark blue eyes twinkled, and Rob chuckled. It was an engaging sound, softening the rather severe impression given by her stark white vet's coat, and dark, workmanlike trousers that she had donned deliberately that morning in order to make herself look as little like a girl as possible, though above the collar her dainty, finely boned face and bright mop of curls would have deceived nobody.

"I've come on legitimate business," Verity Wade excused herself, as she saw Rob glance towards the waiting room door. "And I'm your last customer. I waited for all the others to take my turn," she said virtuously, "so I could stop for a cup of Martha's coffee," accepting the proffered beverage with honest gratitude.

"How is Mel's leg?" asked Martha.

"About ready for use again," said Verity. "I brought him along this morning to see if Miss Fenton would have a look at him."

"Rob," begged Rob.

"Rob it is, then." The fair-haired girl seemed prepared to be friendly. "Hal was too busy to stop this morning when he came to see the cow, and he hadn't got the necessary tools with him in case Mel has to have his plaster off, so he sent me here to see if you would cope."

"I'll have a look," offered Rob, "but who's Mel?"

"This," smiled Verity, indicating a dark collie head that appeared cautiously round the surgery door on hearing his name. "He lost an argument with a cattle truck while we were at Barhill Market some weeks ago. Mercifully it didn't happen until after the lambing was finished, and Hal says he should be mobile again before dipping and shearing. It was a good job Hal was with us at the time," she said thankfully. "I don't know what I would have done otherwise." She snapped her fingers. "Come on in, Mel."

The collie limped forward, and Rob saw that its right foreleg was encased in plaster.

"What a shame!" She held out her hand, and the dog shot a questioning look at Verity.

"All right, old chap, go ahead."

Permission granted, the collie waved its feathery tail, and instantly dropped its muzzle into Rob's hand, much the same as the setter had done the night before.

"You do seem to have a way with dogs, Miss Rob," commented Martha. "Red did the same, last night."

"Red? What, not Hal's setter? Good heavens!" exclaimed Verity, "you are honoured. Why, Red even ignores me!"

"Mel is very obedient," praised Rob, seeking to distract her from the subject. "He asked you first."

"He's a working dog," said Verity Wade practically, "he has to be obedient. But I think he's enjoyed the fuss while he's been out of action," she laughed. "He's getting fat, it's time he went back to work again."

"Let me have a look."

Rob knelt and took the proffered paw on her knee. For the next few minutes she concentrated on her task, her eyes and her fingers busy. The dog sat quietly under her probing, until finally she put his leg to the floor.

"That plaster is ready to come off," she announced. "If you would rather wait for Mr Rand's opinion?"

"I'll give it to you in a few minutes."

Unseen by either of them, Hallam Rand had entered, and stood in the doorway, watching critically while Rob worked. Instantly she stood up, making way for him, and he took her place, kneeling down beside the collie.

"Well, old chap, are you feeling ready for work again?" without hesitation, the dog once again profferred his damaged leg, enduring a repeat performance with stoic patience. "Yes, it's time the plaster was removed," Hal Rand confirmed. "Miss Fenton and I will see to it now."

"It won't hurt him, will it, Hal?"

Verity Wade hesitated, her hands going out to the dog's head.

"Of course it won't hurt him, you goose." The vet's voice softened, and he took both her hands in his. "Clear off into the kitchen to Martha," he told her, pretending sternness, "and make yourself another cup of coffee. Better still, make one for me as well." He reached forward, and gently kissed the tip of her nose. "Now go and do as I say," he commanded. "You can't do anything to help us, and you'll only be in the way."

"At least he makes it sound as if I'm part of the team, if it's only in the guise of a labourer," thought Rob, with an inward grin, gratified nevertheless that he had included her in the general description.

The vet gave Verity a gentle push towards the door, and with the other hand he reached out towards his instrument table. The girl's face blanched beneath her tan, and Rob laid a sympathetic hand on her arm.

"Honestly, Verity, we shan't even pull a hair on his leg."

"Honest?" Relief spread over her face like the sun coming out after a shower.

"Yes. Now go and do as Mr Rand says," said Rob firmly, steering her out of the door.

She shut it behind her, and without waiting for instructions got the dog on to the table. Seeing that she appeared to be sure of what she was doing, Hallam Rand left her alone to do the preparations. Soon afterwards, the collie's leg was free of the plaster, and Rob's left ear was a bright pink where he had occupied his time in licking her while they worked on his leg. Hal Rand smiled at her, briefly. It was amazing what a difference a smile made to his face, thought Rob; he looked all of ten years younger.

"That's one ear you won't need to wash tonight!"

There was cautious approval in his eyes. While she worked, Rob had forgotten the slight nervousness that her doubtful welcome into the house had brought about, and she had become completely absorbed in their joint task, forgetting the presence of the man, her whole attention concentrated in complementing the movements of his hands. Her own deft, gentle fingers slid easily into unison with his own, and the only sound in the surgery was an occasional murmur of encouragement to the patient collie from one or the other of them, bringing a quick response from his feathery tail.

"Now, let's see if he'll use it."

Rand lifted the dog down from the table, and massaged its stiff limb. Rob crossed to the other side of the room and stooped down.

"Come on, Mel." She held out her hand, and Hal Rand released the dog. Instinctively he kept his foot off the floor, and Rob smiled. "No, that won't do. This way, look. Use it, boy," she coaxed. She gave his leg another gentle rub, then stood up and took a step forward, bending over him and gentling his leg into action with her hands to encourage him to follow her. "That's the way. Good boy!" The collie took a couple of steps, then suddenly realising that he could stand on all fours again he danced towards Hal Rand, showing every evidence of delight.

"He's a bit stiff, but that will wear off." The vet looked satisfied. "Verity!" he shouted, opening the door. "Come and look at your invalid."

"Shall I take him through?" offered Rob.

"No." Hurriedly the vet pushed the door to again. "Red is in the kitchen. These two are amicable enough on neutral ground, but. . . ."

"Red would take him apart if he ventured into the house," supplied Verity. "Oh, that looks better. Why, Mel, you've got four legs again!"

The dog danced round the girl, showing off, then he suddenly started to limp on three legs again. Verity's face dropped.

"Oh, Hal!"

"Oh, Mel, you mean. Come here," commanded Rob, amusement in her face and voice. The dog crossed the room to her, walking naturally, and she laughed outright.

"His leg will only hurt him when he wants a bit of attention," she told Verity. "Treat him gently for a

56

couple of weeks to harden the muscles off, and he should have no more trouble."

Verity looked at Hallam Rand, a question in her eyes.

"Miss Fenton is giving you excellent advice," he confirmed. "Don't spoil him, or he'll play up to it." He bent and rubbed the dog's head. "I see I shall soon be redundant in the surgery," he remarked drily.

The laughter drained out of Rob's face, and she flushed painfully. Perhaps she should have waited, and left the after-care advice to him. She had not meant to take charge, though she realised that it might have seemed that way to Hallam Rand.

"I'm sorry—" she began stiffly.

"Sorry about what?" enquired the vet, his eyebrows lifting. "Taking over a difficult surgery that I had no time to attend to myself?"

A furious yapping from somewhere outside saved Rob from replying.

"One of your patients escaped into the garden?" suggested Verity.

"I'll go and see."

Hastily Rob slipped out of her overall, thankful to escape the room and leave the two of them alone. The yapping came from the direction of the rose garden, and she turned towards the mill wheel, guided by the sound. The noise grew to an hysterical crescendo, and Rob found herself confronted by a scene reminiscent of Huckleberry Finn. A small dog of indeterminate breed, bearing more resemblance to a woolly mat than to anything canine, stood on the opposite bank rapidly getting to a point of frenzy at its inability to reach a water rat that was heading unhurriedly towards Rob's side of the river. A small boy, in faded shorts and plimsolls, and almost submerged in a battered straw hat, danced beside the dog, and added a series of whoops to the general din, the while waving a fishing net and jam jar to his own and the dog's imminent peril.

"There he is, miss, right underneath your feet!" he shouted. "Catch him, quick!"

Rob watched, fascinated, as an arrow-shaped ripple headed in her direction.

"Oh, catch him, do! You'll miss him!"

The youngster ran along the bank, pointing desperately with his fishing net, and one end of the long, unwieldy cane caught in a tuft of grass. Unable to stop himself, the boy, complete with hat, tripped over it and somersaulted head first straight into the river. Without stopping to think, Rob kicked off her shoes and dived in. She was an exceptionally strong swimmer, her childhood on the Devon coast had ensured that, and she struck out towards the opposite bank, searching the surface for the boy. His hat floated on the current, bobbing gently towards the mill wheel, and Rob dived deeply, probing the shadowy depths for its owner.

Immediately she left the placid surface water, she realised with dismay the immense strength of the undertow, caused, she guessed, by the pull of the huge mill wheel. For a second or two, panic brushed her with icy fingers as she felt herself drawn inexorably downwards by the current. Then her childhood training asserted itself, and she turned automatically into the flow, exerting all her strength to cleave through it with sure strokes. She caught sight of the child struggling gamely towards the surface, his young arms fighting a losing battle against the downward pull of the undertow. With a supreme effort she caught up with him and grasped him under one arm, kicking frantically for the surface. His added weight hampered her, and it seemed a century before she felt the undertow loose its hold, and she broke surface, gasping.

The boy spat water energetically as she paused for a second or two, treading water, to get her breath back. She gave his bottom a sharp slap.

"Stop struggling, or you'll have us both underneath again!"

Turning, Rob struck out strongly for the bank by the house. It was easy swimming on the top with no current to combat. The child lay quiet in her arms, and soon she hoisted him up the steep bank and on to the lawn of Mill House. He scrambled up in a lively enough fashion, and immediately turned, kneeling towards the stream, his freckled face concerned.

"Will you help Sam up as well, miss? He hasn't got long enough legs to get up the bank."

"Sam? Oh, the dog!" Rob turned to find the woolly mat paddling gamely towards them, its small body fighting the downward pull of its saturated coat. The dog must have come in after the boy, despite its previous caution, for it had made no move to enter the water after the rat.

"I'll go across by the bridge in the garden, and fetch my fishing net and jar," called the child, "if you'll drag Sam out."

He seemed no worse for his ducking, and made off at a trot along the lawn towards the far end of the garden. He was evidently familiar with Hallam Rand's property, and Rob turned her attention to the dog. She swam out to meet him, glad that she had done so, for he was gasping hard. Her fingers found purchase in the long hair, and she dragged him willy-nilly to the bank, and safety.

A pair of slim brown arms reached down, and took the animal from her, and she shook the water out of her eyes to see Verity Wade and the vet kneeling on the bank above her. Hallam Rand looked grim. He gripped Rob's outstretched hands with steel strength, and hauled her up the sheer bank and on to the lawn in one lithe movement. His face was chalk white.

"Of all the crazy things to do!" he gritted. "Have you no more sense than to dive into a mill stream? Don't you realise that the undertow could have pulled you down into the works of the wheel and trapped you under the water? You'd have drowned before anyone could have got to you," he stormed. "And all for a mongrel dog!"

"I can swim well enough," Rob defended herself.

"Not against the pull of a mill wheel, in a river as deep as this," interrupted the vet harshly. He paused for a second, then with icy self-control went on more quietly. "Your concern for animals does you credit, but this is twice in two days that you've placed yourself in jeopardy because of it. While you remain in my employ I would be obliged if you would exercise a little more caution. I have more than enough to do as it is, without having to make arrangements for your funeral!"

"Thank you for getting Sam out." The child trotted back, bearing aloft his fishing net and jam jar, and smiled in an unconcerned fashion at the three grown-ups. "Hello, Mr Rand."

"Jimmy!" The vet gazed down at the boy sternly. "You should know better than to let Sam swim in the stream by the mill wheel. You know full well how dangerous it is. You've been told. . . ."

"But Sam didn't go for a swim. He hates water," protested the lad. "It was only because. . . ."

"Never mind what it was because," broke in Verity hurriedly, with a glance at the vet's set face. "Take Sam with you, and go and sit in my Land Rover, it's right outside the surgery door. I'll take you home." She turned to Rob. "I'll go and look up a kitten for you," she promised.

"Oh, thank you," said Rob gratefully. "I'll. . . ."

"The best thing you can do is to go upstairs and get out of your wet clothes before you catch a chill," interrupted the vet angrily. His cold glance took in her dripping figure, liberally plastered with mud where he had dragged her unceremoniously up the bank. His look reduced her to the age level of Jimmy, and she felt her temper rise.

"If he imagines that I've got no more sense than to go swimming about under mill wheels," she fumed, "he can think what he likes of me! I won't even try to explain!"

Turning her back on him, she ignored the vet completely, and with a curt nod to Verity swung round with as much dignity as her sodden clothes allowed and squelched her way across the lawn and into the house to change.

CHAPTER FIVE

LUNCH was a painful meal.

Rob changed into dry clothing, and sat down opposite to her employer still seething at his overbearing attitude. She was determined not to offer him any explanation for this morning's happening. He could believe of her what he wished, she thought angrily. She had only got to stick the job for a month, and then she would be quit of Hallam Rand and his practice, and all the trouble that her presence at Mill House seemed to bring. It did not occur to Rob to go back on her word and pack her bags before the month was up. The colour of her hair was the badge of a fighter, and she had no intention of being intimidated by the aloof, arrogant, bad-tempered creature who sat opposite her at the table, she told herself forcefully.

"Salt?"

"No, thank you."

matter with her dogs," she added, shaking off her annoyance with an effort. There was no need to let such a trivial incident spoil her day, and she did want to see the village. "It may be that something is really wrong with them, despite the fact that Mr Rand thinks she's a fusspot."

"I'll give you the address." Martha walked out of ~~ dining room with her, and stopped to scribble on ~~~~ ~~d. She tore the top sheet off, and handed

She refused the offered condiment shortly, and he placed it back on the table, his lips drawn to a thin line. Martha placed the last vegetable dish on its mat, straightened it to her satisfaction, and left the room. As the door shut behind her the silence became oppressive, charged with feeling—resentment on Rob's part, and irritation on the vet's. Rob helped herself to as little food as possible, though taking some out of sheer defiance; she would not let the vet see that the episode had upset her appetite. But she tackled her meal with little relish, doing no justice at all to Martha's excellent cooking, and grew angrier as she found each mouthful more difficult to swallow. After the minimum of courtesies to make sure that she had everything she needed within reach, Hal Rand relapsed into stony silence. He glanced across at her once, but her head was bent determinedly over her plate, so he turned his complete attention to his food until Martha came in with the coffee.

"Are there any calls, Martha?"

The query sounded loud in the previously silent room, and Rob jumped, despite herself.

"Only those that you know about, Mr Hal. Oh, except one. Hetty Wilberforce rang and asked if you would go along and look at her terriers some time. She said it wasn't desperate, but she wouldn't say what it was."

"The woman is a fusspot." Rand scowled into his cup. "Miss Fenton can handle it for me. If it's anything that needs serious attention I can go there myself afterwards."

After their amicable teamwork that morning, his remark came like a slap in the face, and Rob's cheeks lost colour.

"I suppose he thinks I'm no good at my job, either," she thought, anger fading into misery. The lunch she had forced down was already beginning to make her feel sick, and she wished she had never come to Mill House. If only she had listened to her mother, and stayed safely at home! She had been happy in the local practice, with people she knew, and with whom either she or her parents were already friends. There was no friendliness here, at least not from Hallam Rand. Instead of the job that she had looked forward to so much, as a good start to her career, she seemed to have chosen an employer who reacted to her every move like a porcupine with all its prickles out.

The silly thought lightened her mood slightly, and she began to feel better.

"Will you give me the address, Martha," she said. "I'll go along there now." She followed Hallam Rand from the table, glad that she no longer need make any pretence at eating.

The vet snapped his fingers for Red to follow him, and made for the door. With his hand on the knob he turned and spoke directly to Rob. His tone was impersonal, professional; he might have been giving her instructions over the telephone, and his grey eyes were cold as if he looked through, not at her.

"Martha knows where to find me if I'm wanted," he told her. "There should be no more calls today, so when you've finished with the Wilberforce dogs you'll

be free to do whatever you choose. Only please," his lips tightened again, "for your own sake, as well as for mine, don't choose to do anything dangerous."

Rob's chin came up, and temper exploded in her eyes. She took an impulsive step forward, but Hallam Rand had closed the door behind him, and the sound of the front door slamming told her that he was out of earshot. The engine of his Land Rover roared and quietened, and the sound of it faded away a road. She f

along the . . . fumed, biting her lip to keep back the angry words that it would be a waste of breath to speak, because Hallam Rand could not hear them.

Martha hesitated, on her way out with the tray of crocks, then she stopped as if making up her mind. "Don't mind Mr Hal, Miss Rob," she said quietly. "It gave him a bad fright this morning, seeing you in the mill stream," she placated. "He almost drowned in it once himself, when he was a lad, and I suppose it brought it all back to him, seeing you in the water. He was fair upset when he came back into the house with Miss Verity."

"Not upset enough to be civil to me at lunchtime," thought Rob miserably.

"I can't imagine him ever being so foolish as to swim in the stream," she said aloud, sourly, thinking that she could not imagine Hallam Rand doing anything foolish, ever. It was only human beings who were foolish, and up to now there had seemed nothing human about him, at least when he was with her. He was different with Verity Wade, of course. "I'll go and see this Miss Wilberforce, and find out what's the

the phone pa...

it to Rob. "Here it is, though it's not necessary, really. You'll find it easily enough," she said. "It's the cottage covered with pink tea-roses, next to the vicarage."

"It sounds as if it might fit its owner," smiled Rob, unwilling to let her vexation spoil her relationship with Martha, who after all had done everything in her power to make her comfortable.

Martha smiled back.

"There are two Miss Wilberforces, not one. Hetty is the fusspot. She's the one who rang. She's short and plump and—and—fluffy," she labelled her triumphantly. "Jane is the other sister. She's older, and taller, and keeps bees. She ought to have been a man."

Rob laughed out loud at Martha's descriptive phrasing, her temper finally evaporating. She could just imagine the two maiden sisters.

She found Martha's description an admirable fit when she parked Hoppy carefully out of the way on the edge of the village green, and walked towards the cottages. The clutter of ducks was still by the pond, but now they slept peacefully on the bank, basking in the sunshine. She gripped the old-fashioned brass knocker, twinkling with polish, and gave a discreet tap.

A chorus of yaps greeted the salutation, and the sound of paws scrabbled on the other side of the door. More than one set, guessed Rob. A quavery, high-pitched voice sounded over the scrabble.

"Go back, both of you—at once! Shoo! Shoo!" The letter box popped open almost on to Rob's nose, with a suddenness that made her jump, and the same voice fluted through. "Wait a moment while I get rid of the dogs."

Rob hoped the intentions of the voice's owner were not as dreadful as they sounded, and she waited patiently until a door slammed somewhere within the cottage, and the scrabbling ceased. A moment later the front door opened, and a small, plump, fluffy-haired woman appeared, and gazed at Rob rather vaguely.

Hetty, guessed Rob correctly. "Miss Wilberforce?" The other nodded. "I'm Rob Fenton, Mr Rand's assistant. You rang the surgery about your dogs."

"Oh, but I rang for Mr Rand." The fluttery voice sounded anxious.

"I know, but he's gone out on an urgent call," lied Rob loyally. Really, she had no idea where the vet had gone to; he had left his whereabouts with Martha, denying her even that amount of trust. "He asked me to call and see what was the matter," she said with a bright smile, smothering the annoyance that the very thought of Hallam Rand generated inside her.

"Oh well, you'd better come in, I suppose." Hetty

Wilberforce opened the door doubtfully, and Rob walked through into a charming little hall.

"Who is it, Hetty?" A loud voice called from the other side of the closed door. "Drat these dogs! Out into the garden, both of you."

Another door slammed firmly, and a second later a tall, angular woman strode into the hall. She seemed to fill it, and towered over Hetty Wilberforce and Rob.

"This will be Jane Wilberforce," decided Rob.

"Is she selling, or collecting?"

"Neither, Jane. It's Mr Rand. . . ."

"Can't be. She's a woman," the other said forthrightly, and Rob stifled a desire to giggle.

"I'm Rob Fenton, Mr Rand's assistant," she explained, with what gravity she could muster. "He asked me to call. I understand you've got a problem with your dogs?"

"They've got fleas," said Jane abruptly, "and it won't be a problem for long—hedgehog fleas don't live on dogs."

"They don't seem quite nice, dear," fluttered Hetty.

"Of course they're not nice," retorted Jane. "They make the dogs scratch. Come through and see them while you're here," she bade Rob. "My sister won't rest until she's got a professional opinion, and paid for it. She won't believe me because I'm free."

She turned, ducking slightly under the door, and Rob followed her, with Hetty bringing up the rear. They entered a tiny, cluttered room, with a small fire burning in the grate despite the warmth of the day. Rob's startled gaze took in the multitude of ornaments that seemed to adorn every flat surface, and she felt sure that this was Hetty's domain rather than Jane's. The latter waved her to a chair, opened a door into the garden, and gave a shrill whistle. Seconds later, two small terriers bounded into the room, with every appearance of perfect health.

One was a cairn. "That's Whisky," introduced Jane. The other was a West Highland White. "That's Soda."

Rob smiled.

"They're in lovely condition, from the look of them," she said, and Jane's rather stern face relaxed.

"They ought to be," she declared gruffly. "My sister feeds them as well as if not better than she feeds us." But her voice held affection.

Rob turned to the dogs. They came to her quite readily, obviously used to nothing but fuss from everyone they met. A quick examination confirmed Jane's diagnosis, and Rob turned to Hetty.

"Your sister is quite correct, they're hedgehog fleas. I should imagine these two rascals have had an encounter with one, and in all probability killed it," she diagnosed. She eyed Hetty's shuddery aversion sympathetically. "They won't live on the dogs, in twenty-four hours they should be gone, but if you like I'll let you have some powder that will hasten their going," she promised, and the plump little woman looked relieved.

"Oh, I would be so grateful. To think they've contracted *fleas*."

She made it sound like smallpox, and her sister snorted.

"All dogs get 'em at some time or another, it's the nature of the beasts." She turned her attention to Rob. "So you're come to help Hallam Rand? He could certainly do with an assistant, the man is run off his feet," she stated.

"If the surgery this morning was anything to go by, I can well believe it," replied Rob fervently. "There wasn't a minute to spare."

"And I suppose you're in a hurry now?"

"Not particularly," replied Rob. "Why, is there something else wrong?" The dogs had looked in the pink of condition. "This is my only call this afternoon," she said candidly.

"Because it's your first day, I suppose. That will soon alter, I expect," said Jane. "Well, while you've got the chance, come along and see our garden, and the bees. You may never have the time again," she prophesied gloomily.

"I'd love to." Rob spoke the truth. Her sore feelings found the uncomplicated friendliness of the spinster sisters a welcome balm.

The garden was as unexpected as Jane herself, and obviously her pride and joy. Rob divided the two sisters accurately into 'house' and 'garden'. A neat vegetable plot climbed a gentle slope on one side, the rows of vegetables as straight as well drilled soldiers, short ones at the front, tall ones at the back, culminating in a thick row of sticked beans. A herbaceous border, dazzling with summer colour, glowed on the other side, and a shallow stepped path meandered between the two, ending in grass among some well laden apples trees. Rob eyed a cluster of white beehives warily.

"They won't hurt you, you know," said Jane, with the confidence of the dedicated. "Go up and take a look."

To Rob's astonishment, Hetty walked calmly past her and slid the top off one of the hives.

"You can see the comb," she encouraged Rob. "They're wonderfully interesting to watch."

Shamed into going closer, Rob sidled apprehensively up to the hive and peeped inside. Several absorbed minutes later she became aware that Hetty still held the top of the hive, and her arms were obviously flagging.

"Oh, I am so sorry," she apologised. "How awful of me to let you hold that heavy lid. But I got quite carried away, watching them." She helped Hetty to place the lid back, and realised to her relief that it was lighter than it had looked. "I quite forgot that I was afraid of bees."

She stepped nimbly back from the hive, her fear returning now that her attention was not distracted, and found herself faced with two beaming smiles.

"We've got a convert, Hetty."

"So we have, Jane." Hetty turned a delighted face to her. "You must try some of our honey, Miss Fenton. I've got a little pot that you can take back with you. And when you get a spare minute, come and help us with the combs. You'll soon lose your fear of being stung," she assured Rob.

Rob had reservations on that score, but she left them unvoiced. The sisters' 'little pot of honey' turned out to be a good half pound, she guessed, and as she thanked them she realised with astonishment that it was gone five o'clock.

"Goodness, I must fly!" she exclaimed. "I must go to the shop for some odds and ends before they close."

She dropped the honey into the front seat of the Austin, and ran back hastily to the bow-fronted cottage that seemed to be shop, post office and general store combined, the only business apart from the public house that the village possessed.

"Hello, miss. Was Mr Rand cross with you for getting wet?"

Rob's small acquaintance of the morning stood at the counter, with a stick of toffee in his hand, and his dog, considerably cleaner for its ducking, drooling at his feet. A slender, fair-haired woman standing beside the boy turned and regarded Rob closely.

"This is the lady that got me out, Mum."

"*Who* got you out, Jimmy," corrected his mother automatically, and held out her hand to Rob. "We owe you a great debt, Miss Fenton. To say thank you doesn't seem enough," she said gravely, and with her other hand she pulled her small son close.

"Mind my toffee, it's all sticky. Oooh, it's gone on your dress!"

"Never mind the toffee, Jimmy," said his mother quietly, to the child's obvious astonishment, and Rob flushed under her steady gaze.

"It was nothing," she protested. "I'm a strong

72

swimmer. But don't go near the mill wheel again, Jimmy," she warned, feeling the lad's eyes on her face. "The tug of the undertow is much too strong for a small boy. Even now, with the river low, it's as much as a grown-up can do to cope with it. What it must be like when there's been a lot of rain . . ." she shivered.

"Mr Rand would have managed all right," defended Jimmy, obviously feeling that the vet was capable of coping with anything.

"Yes," admitted Rob quietly, "but Mr Rand is a grown man, and a strong one."

"Jimmy knows the danger, and he's promised faithfully not to go near the mill stream again," said his mother. "In future he'll fish from the ford across the footpath in the fields at Norton End. It's very shallow there," she explained. "But Tom and I will always be grateful to you for rescuing him. Why not come in some time and have a drink, and let us thank you properly?"

"That's kind of you, Mrs—er—?" Rob realised that she did not know Jimmy's surname, and the other woman smiled.

"I'm Sue Grant. My husband, Tom, is the landlord of the Martyr's Arms, over on the other side of the pond."

"My name is Rob—Rob Fenton. I've come as assistant to Mr Rand—at least temporarily," said Rob ruefully, thinking of the morning encounter with her employer.

"I hope you like us well enough to make it a per-

73

manent appointment," smiled Jimmy's mother. "Don't forget our invitation, will you?"

"I won't," promised Rob. "I'll drop in as soon as I can."

She made her purchases and waved the two good-bye, then made the run back to Mill House without any further mishap with the ducks. Garaging the car, she slipped straight up to her room, then, bathed and changed, made her way downstairs, with the pot of honey in her hand. She hesitated on the bottom step, then turned away from the study door and made towards the kitchen. She did not relish the thought of meeting Hallam Rand before she absolutely had to. In fact, if the opportunity arose she would take her evening meal in the kitchen with Martha. Eating in uncongenial company did nothing to promote good digestion, as Rob had found to her cost after lunch. Anyhow, Martha would be pleased with the honey. She smiled at the thought of the ill-assorted donors, and her face was bright as she opened the kitchen door, and held out her gift towards the housekeeper.

"A present for you, Martha—" she began. A movement by the stove caught her attention, and Hallam Rand looked up from a box on the floor. Rob stopped dead, the smile wiped from her face. For a couple of seconds she stood perfectly still, then she moved forward deliberately and put the pot of honey down on the table. "Jane Wilberforce gave it to me when I went there this afternoon," she said quietly, and turned immediately back to the door, the slender heels of her sandals, the same green ones that she had worn the

74

evening before, tapping sharply on the stone-flagged floor.

"Miss Fenton!"

Rob hesitated, and turned back into the room. However much she disliked the idea of contact with him, Hallam Rand was her employer, and she would not give him the excuse to accuse her of sulking. She had to put up with the job for the rest of the month, and it would be better to do so with at least surface amicability, if nothing else. She eyed him levelly.

"Yes, Mr Rand?"

The vet did not hesitate.

"I owe you an apology for this morning," he said quietly. "Jimmy told Verity what had happened, when she took him home, and she told me when I went to Wade Hollow after lunch for another look at the cow. You undoubtedly saved Jimmy from drowning. I'm very sorry I misjudged you," he said humbly.

Rob could hardly believe her ears. The arrogant Hallam Rand was actually apologising! She stared at him in frank disbelief, poised on her toes like a startled faun, ready to dart away at the first unfriendly move. Becoming aware of the tense silence in the kitchen, she withdrew into herself, and shutters of caution erased the expression from her eyes.

"That's quite all right, Mr Rand. It was a pardonable misunderstanding," she said politely.

She turned to go, and the vet got up from beside the stove quickly, reaching down into the box which he held in his hand.

"Miss Fenton—Rob! Don't go!" He took a step

75

forward. "Verity gave me a peace-offering for you," he said, with a half smile. "I hope you'll accept it, and forgive me?"

His tone was almost pleading, holding Rob against her will. Her eyes searched his face doubtfully, but her ears did not deceive her. He had actually called her Rob! Not the aloof, and somehow disapproving 'Miss Fenton', that made her feel as if she should have her hair screwed back into a bun, like Martha's, and be about as old.

The vet stretched his arm out towards her, and Rob saw that his fingers were curled loosely round something small and black, something that squirmed, and gave a faint squeak.

"A kitten?" She held out her hands, completely disarmed, delight making her face vivid. "Verity knew I was looking for a kitten."

She took the small black bundle in her hands. It was soft and warm, and purring gently like a miniature dynamo. It opened one small blue eye, then shut it again, at peace with its own small world, knowing, as animals do, that the hands that cradled it were friendly.

"So she told me," responded the vet, his finger still stroking the kitten's ears. "I understand that you couldn't treat a cat, so you sought therapy for its owner?"

Rob glanced up at him quickly, uncertain whether this was another rebuke, but his voice held no reproof. She began hesitatingly, still unsure of her ground.

"She's an old lady. She said she lives on her own . . ."

76

"Yes, I know. She'll miss old Ginger." His voice was kindly. "I'm glad you thought to promise her another cat, it will stop her from grieving too much, getting ready for it."

"This one is sweet." Rob cuddled the little bundle of black fur. "It was kind of Verity to send it."

The kitten showed a minute pink tongue in a yawn, and curled up even tighter. Red padded over from the stove, his eyes on Rob's face, and he reached up a tentative paw. His owner gazed at him, astonished.

"Well, I'm blessed! I think he's jealous."

"I could understand that if it was you holding the kitten, Mr Hal," commented Martha. "I really think Miss Rob has brought Red out of his shell, he's never taken to anyone else to my knowledge before. Not even Miss Verity."

It sounded as if the dog took after its owner, thought Rob; they said that dogs usually did. She knelt down and took Red's paw.

"Don't worry, boy, he hasn't come to stay. As soon as I find out where the old lady lives, I'll take him to her. I forgot to get her address," she admitted, vexed with herself for what she was sure the vet would regard as further inefficiency.

"I know the whereabouts of her cottage," said Hallam Rand mildly, with no sign of reproof. "If you like, I'll run you there after dinner," he offered.

Rob looked at him, shocked. The last thing she felt she wanted was his company during the evening.

"If you'll just give me her address, I needn't trouble you," she began. It would be much nicer to run the kitten out to its new owner in the privacy of her own car; she had reckoned on the trip saving her the embarrassment of spending the after-dinner hours at Mill House, where to put it mildly she did not feel welcome.

"It will be no trouble," insisted Hallam Rand.

It seemed as if he was intent on making amends whether she wanted him to or not, thought Rob with an inward grimace, and wished heartily that he would not have such a conscience. Probably Verity had scolded him, she seemed friendly enough.

"It will be an opportunity for you to get your bearings," continued the vet, blandly ignoring her pointed lack of enthusiasm. "Most of the calls about minor troubles from domestic pets come from the cottages. The bigger stuff, the real trouble, comes from the farms." He moved nearer, towering over her. "Now, come and have your dinner." He put his arm round her shoulders, and steered her, kitten and all, towards the door. "You didn't make much headway with your lunch, and if you're going to be of any assistance to me, you'll have to eat properly to keep up your energy."

CHAPTER SIX

THE kitten slept peacefully on Rob's lap throughout dinner. The setter watched her sit down, his amber eyes speculative. As soon as his master was settled in his chair, the dog looked from one to the other of them, and then compromised and curled up on the rug between them.

"As Martha says, you seem to have made a hit with Red."

Rob looked across the table at his owner. "I think he may be just standing guard to see that the kitten does not take liberties in his territory," she said, not sure whether the man would take offence at his dog paying attention to a newcomer who occupied a place at his table on sufferance. But Hallam Rand only smiled, glancing down indulgently at the setter.

"He's an old misanthrope. It will do him good to make friends. Now," as Martha finished serving them, and disappeared through the door, "tell me about your visit to Hetty Wilberforce. You must have made a hit there, too, for them to give you a pot of honey," he said drily. "That's a privilege that's only accorded to the few."

From his tone of voice, Rob deduced that he was not one of the few, and bit back a smile. She told him briefly what had transpired.

"I promised to take some powder along to her," she finished, rather hesitantly. "I know it's not really necessary for hedgehog fleas, but the younger Miss Wilberforce did seem very upset about them."

"Hetty would be," retorted Hallam Rand, and his tone made Rob's heart sink. So much for her promise! Her face must have reflected her feelings, because the man immediately reacted.

"Take her the powder, by all means," he exclaimed, "if you think it will make her happy."

Rob's expression brightened.

"Oh, may I? You really don't mind?" she asked him, her voice betraying her relief. "I'll go and get some from the surgery." She made to rise from the table.

"Sit down again and finish your coffee," commanded her employer, "I've got some powder that will do in the Land Rover. It will satisfy Hetty Wilberforce, and the fleas will go of their own accord," he said, with the ghost of a grin feathering the corners of his eyes.

Rob looked up, his amusement reflecting on her own face, and their eyes met, briefly, with the same rapport that had been so evident when they had worked together removing the plaster from the collie's leg.

They called at the Wilberforces' cottage first, using the kitten as an excuse to get away.

"Hetty will keep you talking all night if you don't," warned Hallam Rand, pinning himself firmly to the driving seat, and refusing to get out. "You take the powder," he told Rob, handing her a packet that looked suspiciously like ordinary talcum. She took it without comment, and her companion met her raised eyebrows with a bland stare. She handed him the kitten to hold, and found him using the end of his good silk tie as a piece of string for its delight when she returned ten minutes later, leaving behind her a happy Hetty, a sardonic Jane, and a renewed invitation to visit them and see the bees as soon as she got a moment free.

"You weren't too long," Hallam Rand commented

when she resumed her seat, and reclaimed the playful little animal. "Now to deliver your bundle." He sucked a scratch across the back of his hand, and rubbed the donor's ears without animosity. "Warn the old soul to watch her chair legs," he told Rob. "That one has got claws like needles!"

He turned the Land Rover out of the village, and they ran for half a mile or so along the lanes before they came to a short row of cottages. The vet pulled up in front of the end one, and handed the kitten down to Rob.

"There's no need for you to hurry away from here, if she wants to keep you talking for a while," he told her gruffly. "She lives on her own. . . ."

"Won't you mind?" began Rob, diffident about the staying power of his newly found good humour.

"I've got my pipe, and Red to keep me company," he assured her, leaning back and beginning to search in his pockets for his tobacco box.

She left him striking endless matches, and he was still smoking with every appearance of contentment when she returned, not quite half an hour later, having installed the kitten with its delighted new owner, inspected a rainbow-hued knitted blanket that she had made for the new arrival, and helped to decide on a name for it.

"We eventually christened it Jet," she announced, returning empty-handed to her seat, to the evident satisfaction of the setter, who inspected her palms to make quite sure that she had not hidden the kitten to tease him.

"You can tell that to Verity," commented the vet. "I want to stop at Wade Hollow on the way back. That is, if you don't mind?"

Rob shook her head, surprised that he had bothered to ask. A few hours ago he probably would not have done.

"How is the cow?" she asked.

"Pulling through nicely now, though I shall keep a close eye on her for a while. Things got a bit sticky first thing this morning," he admitted. "That's why I had to leave you to cope with surgery on your own. Bill Wade—he's the farmer—is building up a pedigree herd, and it would have been a bad setback to him to lose one of his best cows."

"What about the calf?"

"A bull, unfortunately."

The vet pulled the Land Rover up at the gate with the notice 'Wade Hollow' that Rob had passed yesterday, and ran the rails free of the track.

"Let me close it for you," offered Rob, when he had driven through.

"No, sit where you are," retorted her companion. "The track is very rough, and it would spoil your sandals. They're too pretty to ruin," he said, unexpectedly.

Rob raised mental eyebrows, but did as she was told. The track was indeed rough, unfit for high heels, and it carried on for a bone-shaking length of five fields before they jolted to smoother going round the dense belt of trees that she had seen from the hill yesterday, and ran across a smooth, gravelled approach towards one of the loveliest old buildings that Rob had ever seen. What had Mr Wade said? It had been a castle, then a monastery, then a manor house. It had certainly retained a great deal of the charm of each.

A sunken garden, circling the side of what had obviously been an old keep, revealed the one-time presence of a moat, now put to colourful use, and the worked stone cross above the main doorway, flanked by an arch still supporting a bell used long ago for summoning the faithful to prayer, spoke eloquently of the castle's more peaceful successors. Even now, the graceful mullioned windows and bared wall beams spoke more of manor than farmhouse. Hallam Rand glanced at Rob's rapt face.

"You like old buildings, then, Rob?"

"Oh yes," she breathed, "and this one is—lovely."

"I know." He nodded, as if he understood, and shared, her feelings. "This one is mentioned in the Domesday Book, I believe."

"Yes, so Mr Wade said."

"I didn't know you knew Bill Wade?" The vet's eyebrows described an enquiring arc.

"Hardly 'know'," corrected Rob, "he was good enough to—er—set me right on the way here yesterday," she qualified. She saw no reason to enlarge to her employer on the assistance the farmer had given her. Doubtless the vet would only regard the incident as yet another example of female incompetence.

The appearance of Verity Wade, preceded by a gruffly vocal Mel, saved her from the obvious question in the vet's eyes, and she slipped down from her seat, glad of the opportunity to thank the fair-haired girl for the kitten.

"Have another," offered the farmer, appearing behind his daughter. "In fact, have the whole litter," he said generously. "We've got kittens under our feet morning, noon and night here. Verity will play with them in the house," he grumbled goodnaturedly.

"Red might not like it," Rob declined hastily, sure in her own mind that Red's master would not either. She did not feel sufficiently at home at Mill House to introduce a pet of her own, and her stay, in any case, looked like being a short one.

"I thought Red wasn't going to let you out of the Land Rover," laughed Verity. "It seemed ages before you appeared."

"Rob was admiring the house," explained Hallam Rand.

Verity glanced from the vet to his assistant, and Rob saw her eyebrows raise at his use of her Christian name.

"It's wonderfully preserved," enthused Rob hastily, wondering if Verity was jealous. She need not worry, she thought wryly; her present relationship with the vet was more like an armed truce than the beginning of a beautiful friendship.

"You must let me show you round."

A plump, motherly-looking woman, her dark hair going grey, put her arm through that of the farmer, and regarded Rob with a smile.

"Bill told me he helped you on your way yesterday," she said, the smile broadening. "We were hoping you would call. Bill said you were interested in old buildings."

"Oh, I am. You're very lucky to live in one like this," replied Rob, her voice betraying her enthusiasm.

The owners looked pleased, obviously relishing any praise of the home they were so proud of.

"You two go and see the cow." Mrs Wade lumped her daughter and the vet together. "I'll take—er—?"

"Miss Fenton," said Hallam Rand.

"Rob," said Rob.

"I'll take Rob on a grand tour," she promised. "Bring Hal back when you've finished in the sheds, Verity," she instructed her daughter. "I'll have a cup of tea ready in half an hour."

"That means I'd better make it," teased the farmer. "I've never known my wife to get through a tour of inspection in half an hour yet," he warned Rob.

His accusation gained a general laugh from the others, including Verity, who linked her arm through the vet's, and together they made off towards a group of cowsheds on the other side of the farmyard.

Rob turned and accompanied the farmer and his wife indoors, where she spent an absorbed hour going from room to room with her hostess. She was fascinated by the skilful blending of ancient and modern, the clever pressing into service of almost priceless furniture and fittings, so that their beauty was a thing of daily joy to their owners, not relegated to a redundant, museum-like existence, but moulded into an harmonious whole by the tasteful addition of modern pieces, that turned the ancient house into an extremely comfortable home.

"The older things, of course, belonged to my husband's forebears," the farmer's wife told her serenely, "so of course we like to use them for sentimental reasons, as well as for our own convenience. The modern bits and pieces we've added ourselves, but we've been careful to choose only those that could make friends with what we already had," she added with a smile.

Rob appreciated her point. Her comment about furniture 'making friends' revealed a woman with a deep love of her home, and a wish to retain its charm that had been wonderfully fulfilled. The 'bits and pieces', as she called them, also revealed evidence of the wherewithal to indulge that wish, for the additions had been made with more regard to their harmony than their cost.

Rob leaned on an old settle and gazed out of a leaded window that was deeply set into walls nearly two feet thick. The view was superb, looking out straight across the old moat that was now a garden, and filled to the brim with flowers like a huge, circular posy bowl. It made a complete wreath of brilliant colour round the entire house, lending a vivid light to the old walls, and she gave a gasp of sheer delight. Her hostess joined her at the window, her face alight with enthusiasm.

"It's my special hobby," she told Rob. "Before you go, I'll pick you a bunch of flowers for your room. As soon as Verity and Hal come back we'll have a cup of tea, and then you can come and pick where you like. Oh, there they are, just coming now."

Rob followed her pointing finger, and saw the fair-haired girl and her employer emerge from the door of one of the cowsheds. Hallam Rand turned to shut it behind him, and the clack of wood against wood sounded sharply through the open window. Verity turned, waiting for him. She said something, and the vet laughed. He flung his arm across her shoulders, and they strode towards the house, the tall, straight-limbed girl matching her stride easily to his.

"They make a fine couple," thought Rob involuntarily.

Suddenly she felt depressed, curiously isolated in this small, close-knit community, in which she would soon have no part. Like a stone thrown in a pool, that rippled the surface for a while, and then the ripples were gone, and the surface of the water becalmed as if they had never been.

Verity's mother pulled the big window to, leaving a small transom open at the top, shutting out the heady perfume of orange blossom that rose like incense from the sun-warmed garland that caressed the walls. They descended the staircase, built wide enough to accommodate a crinoline, and found the farmer putting the receiver down on the telephone in the hall.

"Who is it, Bill?"

"That fellow from the County Council," retorted her husband, his face grim. "Is Hal back yet?"

"Just coming," the vet called, hearing his name. He appeared through the outer door with Verity. As soon as they were inside he dropped his arms from about her shoulders, and gave her a light spank.

"Go and pour out, it looks as if your father wants to talk shop."

"Not really, we can do it over our cup of tea." Bill Wade ushered him into a side room along with the others, and waited until they were all settled before he satisfied the vet's evident curiosity. "That call was as much for you as for me, Hal. You heard who it was from. Apparently he'd tried to get you at Mill House, and Mrs Main said you would probably be over here."

Martha evidently knew where to find the vet when he went missing, thought Rob. She had said that he practically lived at Wade Hollow.

"You said it was from the County Council."

"Yes, although of course the man was ringing from home at this time in the evening. He guessed he wouldn't be able to get either of us during the day."

"Was the news good?"

"No," returned the farmer shortly, and the vet's face clouded.

"These two are trying to change the law," explained Verity to Rob, settling on the arm of Hallam Rand's chair. "Help yourself," she bade her, passing a plate of feathery-looking sponge across. "It's no use waiting for them to begin when they start riding their particular hobbyhorse."

"What hobbyhorse is that?"

"Bulls in footpath fields," her father answered for her. "You know I told you yesterday that it wasn't against the law in Barshire to run a bull in a field where there's a footpath?"

The vet raised his eyebrows, and Rob felt a momentary vexation. It made it sound as if she had had a lengthy debate over the question, when all she had told the vet was that Bill Wade had set her right on the way to Mill House. Oh well, if he liked to misunderstand, it was up to him. It seemed to be an ingrained habit of his to get hold of the wrong end of the stick, and then belabour her with the other.

"What we're up against," the farmer continued, his tone forceful, "is an ostrich-like County Council. They know the danger of such a ruling, they're all of them country people, some of them landowners themselves, but they either can't or won't put a move on to do something positive about it," he finished bitterly.

"But surely," protested Rob, "no one would be so senseless as to run a bull in a field where there's a public footpath. It's asking for a tragedy!" she cried indignantly.

"If anyone was sensible, the law wouldn't matter," growled the vet. "But there's one farmer in this area who deliberately runs his beast in a frequently used footpath field, simply to be awkward. And someone nearly did get killed, as a result."

"The man wants locking up," the farmer butted in angrily. "And until this senseless law is altered, he'll continue to run the animal there as and when it suits him, knowing that we can't do a thing about it."

Rob raised startled eyes to Verity, hardly able to credit the sense of what she had heard.

"Oh, it's true," the other girl assured her. "One of the people from the village got chased a little while back. If it hadn't been for his dog he might have been badly hurt. As it was, the dog was gored. That's what brought Hal into it, and he and my father have been campaigning ever since to get the law altered. They tried to talk sense to the farmer, but he's the pigheaded type who delights in being awkward, and intends to be a law unto himself. He's a newcomer to the district," said the girl disgustedly, "and he's one that we could well do without."

"And he is?"

"Lewis Ford. He farms a holding on the other side of the village from us," said Bill Wade.

"I shouldn't think many of the villagers use the footpath, if that's what he does."

"Not since the one was chased, they don't. But the trouble is, it's a short cut into the village for any number of people, and of course being by the river it's a pleasant evening walk. Not that it's used any more, unless the walkers have got a nimble pair of heels."

"He doesn't sound a very accommodating type, this Lewis Ford," murmured Rob to Verity, and the girl grimaced.

"He's accommodating all right, in the wrong way," she snapped viciously. "Take my tip, and give him as wide a berth as you would his wretched bull."

Her father scowled.

"Vee had to slap his ears for him when he first came to the village a couple of years ago," he said. "He's steered clear of us at Wade Hollow ever since."

Hallam Rand's face darkened.

"Rob needn't go to his farm at all," he said firmly. "If she gets a call from there, it can be left until I return home. Which we'd better do now," he added, "or Martha will think we've gone missing."

Rob rose instantly, and brought an immediate protest from her hostess.

"You can't go without your flowers. I promised you a bunch for your room."

"Go out on the other side of the house, and walk through the garden to the Land Rover," suggested the farmer. "It's worth seeing," he told Rob proudly. "It's my wife's pride and joy, and it's just at its loveliest now."

"She's seen a lot of it from the windows." Still talking happily about gardening, the farmer's wife led the way, and Rob perforce had to follow, hoping that the vet would not be too put out about the delay. But still, it would give him a few more minutes with Verity; he could not blame her for that.

The garden was indeed a delight. Someone had gentled the sides of the moat so that they were not too steep, and the whole was a living carpet of colour and perfume. A crazy paving path meandered from the bottom to the top of the slope and back again, twisting and turning round clumps of shrubs and herbaceous plants, colourful annuals, summer bulbs, and a riot of pansies and violas that looked as if they had seeded themselves into every odd corner they could find, and grew unchecked, their tiny faces upturned to catch the last of the evening sun, glorying in their own loveliness.

Rob picked her way across the path, trying to avoid stepping on the tiny plants that peeped through the crevices. Inadvertently her foot caught one, and the sharp tang of thyme came to her nostrils.

"Ah! Christmas dinner!"

The farmer's remark evoked a rebuke from his wife.

"He's always thinking of his meals! I'm trying to reduce his waistline, but you'll see I haven't had much success."

"You shouldn't be such a good cook," he defended himself. "Here, let me do that for you."

He reached up to help her with a spray of honeysuckle that she was trying to snap off to add to the bouquet she had already picked for Rob while they wandered. Rob protested that she had already picked enough, and the farmer smiled at his wife.

"She won't believe that anyone can have enough flowers," he teased fondly. "But you've got the Land Rover to take these back in, so don't worry if they're an armful instead of a bunch." He snapped off a spray of double orange blossom, heady with perfume. "There, that will make your room smell nice, that and the honeysuckle."

"What a glorious perfume!" Rob sniffed ecstatically, her enjoyment obvious.

"Verity loves flowers, too," her mother said. "She wants orange blossom for her wedding bouquet. She always said she wanted her flowers to come from the garden at home, rather than from a florist. I think it's a nice idea, don't you?"

"Oh yes," agreed Rob, looking about her. "And she'll have enough to choose from, whatever colour her bridesmaids wear."

She glanced to where Verity and Hallam Rand strolled in front of them. The girl stopped and stooped down, and Rob saw her turn with something in her hand, and tuck it into the lapel of the vet's coat. He reached up and pulled a strand of her hair, gently, teasingly, and they laughed together, and walked on. They were still laughing companionably when Rob joined them by the Land Rover, and turned to thank the girl and her parents for showing her round the old house.

"Come again!"

The invitation came instantly from all three, and with obvious sincerity. Rob did not think there would be much opportunity to accept their invitation, much as she would have liked to, but she kept her forebodings to herself. She only had a month at Mill House, and then. . . . She saw that Verity had picked a carnation for Hallam Rand's buttonhole. It was a clear lemon yellow, its petals making a vivid contrast to the vet's dark jacket. The carnation that he wore at their wedding would be white, thought Rob, and wondered why the perfume of the single acid-coloured bloom should seem to fill the Land Rover, to the exclusion of the armful of flowers that Mrs Wade had given her, and that now rested in the back of the vehicle beside Red.

CHAPTER SEVEN

ROB quickly settled down into the routine of the practice. She was sure of her ground where her work was concerned, and although Hallam Rand kept her under critical observation—prejudiced observation, she called it—she gave him no cause to complain, and the busy days passed quickly. Each morning the surgery was opened promptly at nine o'clock, and it frequently ran late into lunchtime with the waiting room still full. She quickly appreciated why the vet needed a partner, and did her utmost to pull her weight.

While he was working, Rob discovered that her employer was surprisingly easy to get on with. His standards were high, and he spared himself no trouble. It was obvious that he was completely dedicated to his job, and she responded with the best that her training had given her. She found herself slipping easily into his routine, which was very like her own, thorough and conscientious, and although he seemed to accept her help reluctantly at first, as the days went by he began to turn to her more and more.

Without either of them saying anything, it became a habit for them to work together on the more difficult cases, and separately on the routine ones. Rob realised with a feeling akin to awe what a vast quantity of work they had managed, together, to put behind them each day, and she felt a keen sense of pride in her own achievement and part in this. Increasingly Hallam

Rand left the surgery to deal with outside work, and Rob coped on her own.

"I've had to neglect a good deal of that side of the practice," he told her frankly, "and it's been on my conscience. Now I know you can cope with most things here on your own, it will leave me free to catch up with the outside work."

Coming from the man who, on his own admission, was reluctant to employ her, it was indeed an accolade, and she felt quite elated. Perhaps, after all, at the end of the month. . . . But she put the thought from her, disinclined to live in a fool's paradise, and suffer the consequent disappointment when her month's probation was served, and she had to find herself another job. "Probably in some ghastly suburb," she thought dejectedly.

She enjoyed the freedom of working on her own, making her own decisions, and getting to know her patients through their regular visits, and via them, their owners. Rob soon found that she was making a number of friends in the district, and when she did her rounds after surgery was over she was hailed and passed the time of day with by an increasing cross section of the little community. She enjoyed the feeling of belonging, and had to remind herself sternly that she must not come to like it too much, since she would have to leave it all behind her, and start again in a very short time.

The new routine met with Martha's approval as well. She voiced her feelings to Rob when she brought her coffee into the surgery during a welcome breather one morning.

"Mr Rand has gone out," Rob told her, "but he said he would be back in time for lunch."

"These days, when he says that, I know he means it," the housekeeper commented, somewhat grimly. "Before you came, what meals he spared the time for he usually ate standing up, and when he got in for his dinner at night he was mostly too tired to eat it."

"It does seem a busy practice. Too much for one person on their own."

"A great deal too much, as I've been telling Mr Hal for the past year or two," answered Martha roundly.

"Couldn't he have got an assistant before, if he was so busy?" asked Rob, curious to know why he had delayed so long.

"Oh, he advertised," replied Martha, "and one or two came for the post. One even stayed, for a week or two, but he didn't like living so far out in the country. They all seemed to want town life," she snorted disapprovingly, "and so in the end Mr Hal more or less gave up. It's a good many miles to the nearest picture house from here," she acknowledged, "and there was nothing Mr Hal could do about that, so he carried on trying to cope on his own. It was Miss Verity who finally scolded him into trying again," she added with satisfaction, "he just never left a moment to spare for himself."

Rob could well understand Verity Wade's protest. When she married the vet she would not want to have a husband who was continually at work, with never a second to spare for his wife and his home. No wonder she had pushed him into doing something about it while there was still time. And it would have worked, she admitted, if she had only been a man. She herself thoroughly enjoyed living at Martyr's Green, she loved the village itself, and had become enamoured of the countryside around. Now, too, that she had come to know the people, all of them seemingly willing to accept her into their little community, 'except the vet himself', she thought ruefully, she would have been quite happy to settle down and do her part to build up the practice with her employer.

A sudden thought struck her. Could it be that Hallam Rand had another reason for not wanting a girl assistant? Might Verity be jealous of the thought of a close working liaison between the man she intended to marry, and another woman? She did not let the thought disturb her. Her own time at Martyr's Green would not be sufficiently long for any complications to arise in that direction, she thought, and in the meantime the vet's own outspoken reluctance to engage her, and her unfortunate habit of falling foul of him in almost everything except her work should be quite enough to convince Verity that she stood in no danger from her direction.

Verity popped in one morning with some eggs for Martha, and stopped for the inevitable cup of coffee that seemed to be a long-standing habit with her as soon as she appeared at Mill House.

"Are you coming to the dance?" she enquired of

Rob. "What will you wear?" Her interest was both feminine and friendly.

"Dance? What dance?" It was news to Rob that there was one.

"Oh, hasn't Hal told you?" the other girl exclaimed. "It's the village garden fête at the weekend, and there's always a hop in the church hall afterwards. You must come," she urged, and her invitation sounded quite genuine. "Of course you will. Hal will bring you." She waved aside Rob's doubtful murmur. "There'll be a crowd of us together, you'll be sure to enjoy it."

Rob was sure she would. She loved dancing. But she was not so sure that she liked the thought of going with Hallam Rand. To start with, there was Verity. The vet might not be so keen to escort his assistant as well as the girl he was to marry, and Rob had no desire to make an unwanted third. She felt that, already, in Mill House without making matters worse.

"Does Mr Rand go to the fête as well?" she hedged, her imagination boggling somewhat at the thought of her rather austere employer enjoying the bucolic delights of a village garden fête.

"Of course," replied Verity, looking surprised. "He has the job of judging the dog show, so he's got to be there. You must bring along your pennies and have a go at the hoop-la," she smiled, downing the rest of her coffee and sliding off her seat on the edge of the table. "Tell her, Hal," she commanded the vet, who appeared unexpectedly through the door of the surgery, and started to rummage in the cupboard where they kept the stock of drugs.

"I came back for some more injections. Have you used them all, Rob? Oh no, here they are." He dived his hand into another shelf and fished out a carton. "I'll take half of them. Order another lot from the supplier, will you?"

Rob nodded, and made a note on her pad. The vet pocketed the handful he had retained, and turned towards the door. Verity sidestepped in front of it, and blocked his way.

"The fête," she insisted, "and the dance afterwards."

The vet's eyes crinkled into a smile.

"What about them?" he countered teasingly. "They're several days away yet. Why worry about them now?"

"I told Rob you would bring her," the girl told him frankly. "She hasn't been to a do in the village yet. I don't think there's been one since you've been here," she said to Rob. "It would be a pity to miss this one."

"In other words, come while you still have the chance," thought Rob bitterly. Verity obviously knew that she would not be at Martyr's Green long enough to come to the next one. Just the same, she had no wish for Hallam Rand to feel obliged to escort her to the fête, or to the dance in the evening. Doubtless he would want to take Verity himself, and would hardly welcome being pushed into escorting his assistant.

"I don't think . . ." she began hesitantly, and Hallam Rand butted in.

"Don't you like dancing, Rob?"

"Oh yes," said Rob, "but. . . ."

The vet eyed her slender figure, formal in its surgery overall, and smiled briefly.

"Then we must make sure there are no calls to occupy us on Saturday," he told her. "Verity is never sure of me turning up," he explained. "If she's shang-haied you into going against your wishes, as a surety for me, you must say so."

"Then that's decided," said Verity firmly.

She gave Rob no time to answer. "No time to refuse," Rob thought, though she would have liked to. She did feel that she had been pushed into going, and had put the vet in a position where he would have had no option but to turn up. She felt thoroughly uncomfortable, and vexed with Verity for her rather obvious ploy, but she could not very well back out now. She watched them go out together, and turned to tidy up the drugs cupboard with a feeling of depression.

"I need a break," she decided, so as soon as her calls were done—she only had two that afternoon—she searched out her camera and made her way to the village green to try and get some shots while the light lasted. The afternoon was clear and bright, and she took several snaps of the church, and the cluster of cottages, from different angles, and one of the Martyr's Arms from beside the duckpond.

Shifting her position slightly to take in the sleeping group of ducks, she became aware of a figure crossing the field of the viewfinder. She waited for a second or two, engrossed in her task, expecting the person to carry on walking. Instead he turned deliberately and came towards her, until soon she had a close-up in her viewfinder of a dark, swarthy face, surmounted by an untidy mop of black, curling hair, greasily clinging to the open collar of a non-too-clean shirt.

"Take me. I might add a bit of local colour."

Rob stiffened, and a flush of annoyance stained her cheeks.

"I've taken all I need, thank you." Deliberately she snapped her camera shut, then hesitated as she saw Jimmy running across the green towards her, with Sam panting in his rear. She would have liked a snap of the little boy and his dog, he was a likeable youngster.

"Hello, Jimmy!"

"Hello, Miss Frenton." He gasped to a halt. "Mum sent me across to ask if you could spare the time to come in for a cup of tea." His glance went across to the dark-haired man who still stood confronting Rob. "Miss Fenton is working for Mr Rand," he said. "She's a vet." He threw the information at the man as if he had a purpose, and his young voice made it sound curiously like a threat.

"So you work for Hallam Rand?" The coarse features darkened. "Well, you can tell your boss from me. . . ."

"Come on, Miss Fenton, let's go. We've got cream cakes!"

Jimmy tugged at her hand urgently, and Rob turned, unsure of what it was that she had to tell Hallam Rand, but quite sure that she did not want to either hear the message, or deliver it. Her relationship with her employer was balanced on a knife edge as it was, without interfering in what looked like a misunderstanding between these two. The vet seemed good at misunderstandings, but for once Rob felt her sympathy on his side. She did not like the look of the slovenly creature in front of her, and seeing that she had no intention of listening to him he hesitated, shrugged, and shambled away towards an incredibly dirty and battered old jeep on the other side of the village green. Rob noticed to her horror that his walk was not quite steady.

She laughed, half with relief, and allowed the boy to tug her across the green towards the Martyr's Arms, the woolly Sam leading the way, evidently as keen as his small master at the thought of the treat in store.

"How do you tell which end is which?" she chuckled, regarding the dog later from her seat beside the landlord, in the low-ceilinged living room at the inn.

Tom Grant laughed.

"One end eats, and the other wags," he smiled. "Someone dumped him when he was a puppy. Some holidaymaker, I imagine." His tone betrayed his opinion of people who callously dumped animals.

"And we took him in," supplied his wife, plying Rob with another cake.

"I'm going to enter him for the dog show," Jimmy announced proudly. "That ducking he had gave him a bath, and if I brush him up a bit. . . . Do you think he'll get first prize, Miss Fenton?" he asked hopefully, and Rob forced back a smile.

"He's in a class of his own, Jimmy," she assured the proud owner, and hoped that something could be done on the day of the fête so as not to disappoint the bright little face in front of her. She would try and mention it to Hallam Rand, though she supposed that would be cheating in a way. Anyhow, she decided, she would broach the subject with her employer when the opportunity arose. There was a day or two to go yet, the fête was not until Saturday.

The opportunity did not arise that evening, and during the next hectic morning Rob forgot all about it. The surgery was full, and she had the added task of answering the telephone as well, because Martha had gone into Barhill to do some shopping.

"I'll be back about four," she told Rob. "If you have to go out, just leave a note on the hall table where you are in case any calls come while you're away."

"Right-ho!" Rob responded cheerfully, donning a clean white coat in readiness for the morning's work.

"You can get me if you want me at the County Council offices," Hal informed her in his turn. "The number is on the pad."

"At least he's beginning to trust me with the knowledge of his whereabouts," thought Rob, and remembered belatedly that as Martha would be out of the house anyway, he had no option but to leave the information with her.

"If it's about bulls in footpath fields, then I wish you luck," she said feelingly.

He glanced at her quickly, a look of pleased surprise on his face.

"So you remembered? We could do with more people of your frame of mind in the Council offices," he said, with emphasis. "If you're ready now, Martha," he called through the kitchen door, "I can run you into Barhill and save you waiting for the bus."

The door slammed behind them, and Rob immediately became absorbed in surgery tasks. She had three telephone calls during the morning, none of which required a visit; one wrong number, and then Hetty Wilberforce rang to explain at length that the powder Rob had brought had 'worked like a charm'. "There's no trace of fleas at all now, Miss Fenton. I'm so grateful," she fluted. "With the dog show on Saturday and all."

Rob, in the middle of stitching a cat's shoulder, had to explain that she was occupied in the surgery, whereupon her caller spent another precious five minutes apologising profusely for disturbing her, before she rang off.

It was long gone one o'clock before Rob closed the door on the last of her patients with a sigh of relief, and reached for the thermos of coffee that Martha had thoughtfully left for her. It was hot and strong, and she wrinkled her nose at the sharp, sweet tang of it. The telephone rang again as she lifted the cup to her lips.

"Mr Rand's surgery."

"Norton End farm here." The voice on the other end of the line was brusque, rough. Rob thought she had heard it somewhere before, but she could not quite place it. "I've got a cow in some trouble. I want someone out here right away."

"I'm on my way," promised Rob. "But first tell me what's wrong."

But the line had gone dead. She put the receiver down, and reached for the telephone book, then realised that she did not know the name of the farmer. Her eyes sought the large-scale district map hung on the wall of the surgery. Norton End was on the other side of the village, backing on to the Martyr's Arms. She would be there almost as quickly as she could phone.

She reached resignedly for her bag, visualising a hundred different things that could spell trouble to a cow, and hoped that her admittedly comprehensive emergency kit would cope with whichever one it happened to be. If only Martha had been in the house she could have discovered who the farmer was, and phoned him back, but by the time she had searched the information out she would be on the spot anyway. She shrugged her shoulders and quitted the surgery, locking the door carefully behind her. She would just leave a note for Martha on the telephone pad, to tell her where she had gone. She bent and scribbled 'Norton End farm, cow in unspecified trouble' on the top sheet, and searched out Hoppy from the garage. Soon she was bowling into the village, past the church. They turned left into the lane that ran at the back of the Martyr's Arms, and followed it along the course of the River Bar.

She caught sight of Jimmy and his dog beside the water. She tooted her horn, and the boy looked up, his fishing net raised in instant greeting as he recognised the Austin, and Rob assumed that he was on his way to the ford to fish. His mother had said that it was shallow there. The dog Sam scuffled backwards and forwards round the boy's feet, and Rob smiled to herself. Another ducking via the ford might even get him into show condition for the garden fête, she thought, and remembered that she had not said anything about it to the vet yet. If he was not too absorbed with the results of his meeting at the Council offices, she would try and make the opportunity tonight, depending on what mood he was in when he came back. Although the atmosphere was more amicable between them now, she was still unsure of her position, and reluctant to upset him again.

She waved back to Jimmy, and carried on alertly along the lane, looking for the farm entrance. She could see the buildings in the distance; there must be a track leading off the lane soon. Eventually she ran right past it, and only realised that her brief glimpse of a sagging gatepost, minus a gate, had included what looked like a notice. It was.

The roughly painted letters were faded to the point of only being half visible, and the single nail that held it had worked loose, so that the notice itself teetered on the end in imminent danger of disappearing into the tangle of thicket that sprang up all round the rotting post. The gate itself lay flat on the ground, half obscured in a riot of nettles and bramble, obviously its home for several seasons. Curls of rusted barbed wire, sprung dangerously back from the rotted posts that once held them, abdicated their duty as gap fillers in the unkempt hedge. Rob mentally compared the entrance facing her with the well oiled barrier barring the entrance to the track leading to Wade Hollow, and found the Norton End farmer, whoever he was, definitely wanting.

She turned the Austin on to the weed-strewn track and chugged along in second gear, hoping that it would not prove to be the five fields length of the one to the Wades' farm. It was infinitely rougher, and the springing of her car, already feeling its years, was not on the same purpose built level as the vet's Land Rover. In fact, the track petered out after three thistle-strewn fields, and ended in front of a dilapidated-looking building that Rob had difficulty in deciding whether it was house or barn.

At the sound of her engine in the yard, a woman appeared at the door, wiping her hands on a dirty-looking calico apron. Lank, mousy hair, untidily escaping from a carelessly applied rubber band, wisped unheeded about her face as she eyed Rob suspiciously.

"Well?"

"I ought to be used to this sort of welcome by now," thought Rob wryly. "It doesn't look as if women vets are popular with the profession, or their clients." She introduced herself.

"I'm Mr Rand's assistant. You rang to say you had a cow in some sort of trouble."

"Well, it's no use you coming to the house. The cow's in the shed over yonder."

The woman pointed towards a broken-down-looking shed with a sagging roof, standing—if so it could be described—about forty yards beyond the back of the house.

"I'll find my own way," offered Rob, but the woman did not wait to hear her out. She turned her back and re-entered the house, shutting the door uncompromisingly behind her, and Rob heard the clatter of a pail as if she might have been in the middle of scrubbing the floor.

Left to her own devices, Rob picked her way across the farmyard to the shed on the other side. The woman's manner had been abrupt to the point of rudeness, but she could not stop to worry about that now. She carefully skirted a rusty disc harrow lying, like the gate, in a bed of nettles, and her critical gaze took in the general air of seedy neglect that hung heavy over buildings and yard. Her opinion of the farmer dropped to zero. Gingerly she stepped through a clutter of depressed-looking fowls, all showing evidence of feather-pulling, and reached for the shed door, half afraid to pull at it too hard in case it came away from its hinges in her hands. It swung out creakily, catching on the deeply rutted earth outside, and she left it open to let in a bit of light. After the bright sunlight outside, the interior of the shed seemed dark, and she paused for a minute to let her eyes adjust to the gloom.

Something moved in the one corner, and her eyes took in the shape of a small cow. "A runt," thought

Rob. "It would be, on a holding like this." The animal was tethered loosely by a much knotted piece of binder twine, and it eyed her as she moved across to it, talking quietly while she walked. It chewed its cud with bovine patience, its jaws moving up and down with a rhythmic sound that in a better cared for animal always left Rob with a strange sense of peace. It was such a quiet, meditative occupation, it was a pity human beings did not do the same, she thought; there would be fewer nervous breakdowns if they did.

She was glad that she had left the door open. Even now, the light in the shed was poor. True, there was a window of sorts, but it was partly stuffed with dirty sacking to mend a break, and what glass was left was so obscured by grime and cobwebs as to be virtually useless for letting in any light. She looked round the shed. There was only the one animal inside, indeed there was only room for the one amid the general clutter littering the floor. Her practised eye told her that it was in calf, but it did not seem to be in any distress. She ducked underneath its neck, running her hands across its spine gently, looking for the reason she had been called out. She soon found it. A jagged rip across the animal's shoulder spoke eloquently of an encounter with barbed wire, and Rob remembered the rusty tangle in the hedge by the gateway. She ducked back underneath the beast's neck, and started to untie the rope from the ring in the wall.

"I shall have to take you outside, old girl," she addressed herself to the cow. "It's too dark to be able to attend to you in here."

She got the knot untied at last, and turned the cow towards the door. There should be something she could tie it up to again once she was outside. She wished the farmer would put in an appearance; it would make things better for her if he were there to steady the animal while she worked.

"What are you taking my cow outside for?"

A surly voice growled at her from the doorway, and she recognised the tones of the man who had phoned her earlier. "I tied it up in here to keep it still while you looked to the rip in its shoulder."

"I can't possibly see to work in this shed, it's much too dark." The man was standing with his back to the open doorway, blocking the light, his face in the shadow. "Let me through, and I'll attend to it outside." Rob did not wait for him to answer, but straight away turned the cow into the doorway, obliging him to move. Once outside, she looked round for somewhere to tie it to, but there seemed nothing handy except the latch of the door, and one good pull from the cow would assuredly bring the door down, she suspected, and probably the shed with it. She turned to the cow's owner, and found herself confronting the dark, scowling face that had filled her viewfinder on the village green the day before. Her second encounter did nothing to improve her first impression of the man, and her face tightened. "Please hold the rope, so I can start work."

She held it out to him, and he took it with a surly grunt, but he held the cow still while she opened her case and got out her equipment. The rip was a bad one, and as she worked she seethed, longing to give the farmer the tongue-lashing he deserved for allowing the animal to get into such a state.

"This wouldn't have happened if you'd cleared up the old barbed wire on your property, Mr—er—" was all that she allowed herself. She did not want to get involved in a row with one of her employer's clients, and risk further trouble when she reported the case to him that evening.

"I ain't got time to pretty the place up." His scowl grew blacker. "And my name's Ford—Lewis Ford," he informed her, with a glare that suggested she should have known all along.

Lewis Ford! The man who kept his bull in a field where there was a footpath. Rob could well understand, now, why Verity had called him an awkward type. He and his wife both seemed tarred with the same brush, she thought. She threaded a needle and glanced up at him, her voice coldly professional.

"Hold the animal a bit more firmly, will you? I'm going to have to stitch the rip here."

She went about her work, ignoring him completely. Her fingers were unhesitating and sure, and she finished her stitching unhurriedly, taking time to check over her handiwork to see if it needed further attention. It did not. The shoulder was neatly dressed, and the cow stood calmly enough, apparently undisturbed by its unpleasant experience.

"That should heal all right. Either Mr Rand or I will call again in a day or two, just to make sure. If there's any sign of infection before then, give me a ring," she bade the farmer.

"There hadn't better be," the man snapped. "If you've done your work properly, it shouldn't need another visit from either of you."

Considering that the rip in the cow's shoulder was due to his own carelessness about his fences, Rob felt that his abruptness was a bit uncalled-for, even though he was at odds with her employer over allowing his bull free access over a public right of way.

"No, but it might . . ." she began, anxious for the wellbeing of the beast.

"And it might not," he growled back. "The less I see of either you or your boss on my land, the better." His hand shot out and gripped her arm in a vicelike hold. "I don't want no nosey-parkers ferreting about Norton End, and you can tell that to Rand when you see him!"

Rob gasped. Pain shot up her arm from the cruel grip of his fingers, and she winced.

"Let go of her, Ford. At once!"

A voice, dangerously quiet, spoke from behind the farmer, and the man loosed her arm and spun round. Rob rubbed it, feeling the pain of the blood flowing back now that the pressure was taken away, and she turned to confront the vet. His face wore a scowl as black as Lewis Ford's, and when he spoke to her his voice was cold.

"Put your things back into your case, and go back to your car," he commanded her.

"I was just checking to see if there was anything else...."

"I'll check for you," he retorted grimly. "Do as I say."

His voice brooked no disobedience, and Rob hastily stuffed her things back into her case, careless of tidiness, and turned away. She did not look at the farmer again, but deliberately turned her back on him and slipped thankfully into Hoppy's lumpy front seat.

"Phew! He's a bad-tempered type, and no mistake," she informed the Austin—and then wondered which of the two men she meant.

A strong hand grasped the handle of her passenger door and wrenched it open. She spun round, her eyes wide, but it was only the vet.

"You left this." He held out a bottle of ready diluted disinfectant, and she opened her mouth to thank him. "Perhaps in future," he interrupted her, thrusting the bottle forcefully into her hand, "you'll take some notice when you're told not to have anything to do with a person. Verity told you what type of man Lewis Ford was, and I said you were not to answer calls from him. Now start your car, and I'll follow you home."

CHAPTER EIGHT

"HE thinks I came here deliberately!" Sheer shock froze Rob to her seat, and she stared after Hallam

Rand disbelievingly as he strolled towards his Land Rover. "He thinks I knew which holding Lewis Ford farms, and came here despite what Verity said. He must think I came for a cheap thrill." The vet had seen the man grab her arm, and put the wrong interpretation on his action. Hallam Rand had been too far away to hear what the farmer had said, and there had been no time to explain, indeed he had not given her the chance.

"Perhaps in future you'll take more notice."

The cool tones had stung the angry colour to Rob's cheeks, and hot temper rose in her throat. She glared furiously after the vet's retreating figure. The Land Rover door slammed behind him, and he turned in his driving seat and looked in her direction. She stared back in mute anger. He waited for a few seconds, and then slid down his window and called out to her.

"Can't you start it?"

"Start it?" The sound of his voice brought Rob off the boil, and she shook herself back to reality. "Of course I can start it!"

She was so vexed that she had almost forgotten she had to drive herself back to Mill House. Hallam Rand had called it 'home', but she could not think of it as that. Her hand shook slightly as she reached for the ignition key, and Hoppy started up instantly, as if glad to be leaving Norton End farm. She stamped angrily on the accelerator, and the little Austin caught a bad bout of kangaroo petrol. With three startled leaps it cleared the rutted farmyard, and the resulting jolts shook Rob back to herself again.

"Sorry, Hoppy, I shouldn't take it out on you," she apologised, quietening down, and proceeding more sedately along the apology for a drive. "The track is rough enough in all conscience, without me making it worse."

The brief mechanical struggle had steadied her, and she drove smoothly back to Mill House and garaged the Austin with a sigh of thankfulness. She still felt angry, but now it had simmered to a dull ache, and suddenly she felt she wanted to cry. She entered the house through the back way rather than face the vet again, but she need not have bothered, for she heard him talking on the phone through the open study door. She turned towards the stairs, but was forestalled by Martha.

"There's a cup of tea poured out in the kitchen, Miss Rob. Come along and get it while it's hot," she bade her cheerfully.

It was not an unusual invitation at this time in the afternoon if she happened to be in the house, and Rob turned towards her instantly, suddenly urgent for a sympathetic ear. She curled up in the big rocking chair beside the kitchen stove, and accepted the hot, strong brew that was the housekeeper's speciality. She shook her head at the proffered scones, an unusual refusal that brought a crease of concern to the kindly face opposite to her, but even to please Martha she could not eat one now. She felt as if food would choke her.

"It's a coincidence, you and Mister Hal getting in together," commented the housekeeper happily. "It will save having to make another pot of tea later on."

"It's no coincidence," replied Rob wearily. "Mr Rand turned up at Norton End farm just as I'd finshed stitching up a cow, and he followed me back."

"Norton End? What, not Lewis Ford's place? I wouldn't have thought Mister Hal would have let you go there," Martha clucked disapprovingly. "Lewis Ford is a rough, uncouth sort. Better you'd stayed away, though of course if you were helping Mister Hal that would be different."

"I wasn't helping him. He came afterwards. And Verity did warn me about not going to Lewis Ford's place, but the trouble was she didn't say which holding he farmed. I wasn't to know that he and Norton End went together." Rob stretched out her cup for a refill, and Martha caught sight of the marks on her arm, already beginning to show signs of bruising.

"Don't tell me he . . ."

"No, he didn't. He was merely making sure that I stayed to listen to what he had to say. I met him on the green yesterday, by accident, though of course I didn't know who he was then. He wanted to give me a message for Mr Rand then, but he wasn't completely sober, so I walked away. He evidently intended to make sure I listened today." Rob rubbed her arm ruefully. It ached where the man had gripped her.

"And what message did he have for me today?"

Hallam Rand had come silently into the kitchen, his rubber-soled shoes making no sound on the quarry floor, and both the women jumped.

"Well?" The vet's voice was grim.

"He said—he said to tell you that he didn't want any n-nosy parkers ferreting about Norton End. I think he meant about his bull." Rob's voice trailed away lamely, unable to continue. Misery stopped her throat. Nothing she did seemed right for Hallam Rand. For a little while she had hoped, but after this she was sure that he would stand by his first decision, and refuse to renew her appointment at the end of her month's stay. She leaned back in the chair, defeated, and closed her eyes against the threatening tears. She heard Hallam Rand speak to Martha, heard him go out of the room, and felt Martha's motherly hand brush across her hair.

"Don't let it worry you, dear. Mister Hal will go and check up on the cow, whether Lewis Ford wants him to or not. You won't have to go there again."

"He thinks I went there deliberately."

She no longer felt angry at the injustice of it, only unhappy that it had to be this way, that her shining hopes had turned to dust at her every move. And it did not help that none of the misunderstandings she had had with her employer, except the initial one over her name, was her own fault.

"I'm sure he thinks nothing of the sort." Martha sounded scandalised.

"He certainly does not." The vet had re-entered the kitchen, and now stood regarding his white-faced assistant intently. "It seems as if Verity and I were partly to blame," he said. "All the locals know what a surly brute Lewis Ford can be, it never occurred to me that a stranger wouldn't know which farm he belonged to. When I told you not to take any calls from there, the thought never entered my head."

Rob looked up at him, her too bright eyes glistening darkly, like the bark of a beech tree wet with rain.

"I thought—you thought. . . ." She could not go on.

"I thought nothing of the kind," snapped the vet, then amended his tone hastily as Rob's mouth drooped. "Which brings me to something I've meant to say for the past fortnight."

"Here it comes," thought Rob, and braced herself for the news that she knew must come. Evidently the vet did not intend to wait until the month was up.

"Yes?" She tried unsuccessfully to put a dignified firmness into her tone, and failed lamentably.

"In future," the vet commanded her, "whenever you go out on rounds, you must always take Red with you."

Rob sat up and stared.

"Take Red?"

"Take Red." The vet's voice was adamant. "And don't look at me like that. He won't bite. At least, he won't bite you." He paused for a moment, studying her thoughtfully, and then went on, "I'm not happy about you wandering the countryside on your own like this. This area is very isolated, and I should feel a great deal easier if I knew you always had the dog with you."

Martha stared at her employeer, amazement writ in an almost ludicrous fashion on her face, a reflection of Rob's own expression.

"You, leave Red behind? I don't believe it!"

"I'm afraid you'll have to," the vet told his house-keeper crisply. "There's nothing I can do about providing Rob with a human escort." He ignored her indignant "I'm quite well able to look after myself!" and went on, "Short of confining her to treating lap-dogs and pet cats around the village, there's no other way of accepting her services. And there are not enough lapdogs and pet cats to keep you occupied in these parts," he smiled. Swiftly, he knelt down beside her chair. "No, don't get up," as she started to rise. "Just sit still while I rub some of this ointment on your arm." Evidently he had fetched it when he quitted the kitchen. He unscrewed the top off a jar of pink-coloured cream, and dipped his index finger into it. "It doesn't smell, and what's good for healing bruises on small animals won't hurt your skin, either." Gently, very gently, he smoothed the cream across the swell-ings. It was cool, and comforting, and Rob relaxed under his touch. Thank goodness he did not think she had gone to Norton End the moment his back was turned. She shivered, and the look in the man's eyes above her grew steely. "Does it hurt much?"

"Oh no, hardly at all. That's wonderfully comforting."

And so was his evident belief in her integrity. She felt immeasurably relieved. She could not imagine why she should care so much what he thought. She only knew that she did. Pride, I suppose, she thought wryly. Hal Rand's voice broke in on her musings.

"You must promise me never to leave Red behind

when you go out," he insisted. "In a city practice it wouldn't matter, but out here. . . ."

He spoke as if he intended to keep her services until the month was up, and suddenly Rob had to be sure.

"You mean I can stay?"

Rand looked surprised.

"Of course. You haven't been here the month yet."

"I seem to have done enough up to now," she admitted ruefully.

"You certainly have," he replied fervently, and his tone changed. "We've done more working together than I would have believed possible, in so short a time. But you must promise. . . ."

"Oh yes, I promise I'll keep Red with me. That is, if he'll stay."

Somewhere inside her, something started to sing.

"If he won't," said Hal, "I'll go out and buy the biggest bull terrier I can find, and train him for you."

"Red would certainly object to that."

Rob laughed, shakily, and straightaway felt better.

"Martha, I think I'd like that scone after all."

"Don't feed her too many, Martha," commanded Hal Rand, rising to his feet. "Verity and her parents are coming to dinner, remember, and if she can't eat they'll think I starve her. As well as beat her." His glance went to her arm.

"I'll cover that up."

Rob rose, her hand instinctively going up to her bruised arm, feeling the pull of the creamed area against her fingers. It still tingled to the vet's touch, firm, yet amazingly gentle. Not crude and brutal, like that of the farmer at Norton End. She hesitated.

"If you're having guests for dinner, I could have mine in here, with Martha—" she began, not sure whether the vet would want the company of his assistant when he was entertaining his personal friends. They had been kindness itself to her when she went to Wade Hollow, but a dinner at home was rather a different affair. He and Verity might prefer just family company, and her presence would make for odd numbers anyhow.

"Certainly not!"

"The very idea!"

The vet and his housekeeper spoke simultaneously.

"You'll have your dinner as you always do, with me," Hal told her, and his voice brooked no argument. "Now cut along upstairs and get ready, there's nothing more for you to do here tonight."

Normally Rob spent the hour before dinner attending to the surgery records, but evidently her employer thought otherwise this evening, and she was grateful for his consideration. She would take a quick lie down before she came downstairs, there was plenty of time, and she wanted to feel fresh if Verity and her parents were coming. Doubtless the farmer wanted to hear how the vet had got on at the Council Offices during the morning. It would be pleasant to see them again, but the singing inside her quietened a little. It would have been nicer still to have had dinner with just the two of them and Red, and a quiet evening afterwards.

"How did you get on at the Council Offices this morning?" she asked, on her way out.

"Not much progress." He sounded exasperated. "They're like the mills of God, in those places. They grind slowly." He paused with his hand on the study door. "You'll hear all about it when I tell Bill Wade this evening," he promised her, and with that she had to be content until dinner time.

She chose a white silk blouse with long bishop sleeves as being about the coolest thing she had got that was still capable of hiding her bruised arm, and teamed it with a floor-length black skirt. She left the neck of the blouse open, shirt-style, and linked it loosely with a plain gold necklet band that had been a gift from her parents on her birthday. The stark simplicity of the outfit suited her, highlighting her own natural colouring so that her bright hair seemed even brighter by contrast. She brushed it flat against her head, into a neat halo of copper against her delicately boned face, and it stayed obediently where she put it except for one soft curl that would insist on rolling down over her forehead. She brushed it back impatiently, but it tumbled back again on to her eyebrow, as if it wanted to peep into her eyes, and read the secrets that might lie there. She frowned, hesitating whether to wet her brush and plaster it back, but there was no time for that now. She did not use grips, her hair never needed setting, and it was too short to need restraint normally. Rob tossed the brush down on the dressing table and gave it up. It would have to do, she thought. It was not as if she were going to a dance where it might get in the way, it was more or less a family dinner party, at least as far as the vet was concerned. The thought made her feel more than ever an outsider, although the topic of conversation that took precedence at the dinner table drew her in equally with the others.

Bill Wade listened patiently to what the vet had to tell him of his visit to the Council Offices that morning, and his expression said that he was not impressed.

"I told Rob they're like the mills of God," said Hallam Rand.

"These don't grind slowly, they grind to a halt," growled the farmer. "I'm beginning to wonder if there's not some sort of higher authority we can appeal to, Hal. Some kind of Ombudsman, for instance?"

"These people are on the County Council, Bill," retorted the vet. "And they do have the last say where County laws are concerned. You know that."

"I suppose so," answered the other grimly. "Lewis Ford knows it, too, unfortunately."

Rob glanced up quickly at her employer, but his attention was turned to Verity, and he made no mention of what had transpired that morning. She heaved a small sigh of relief, and helped herself to vegetables.

"It's nothing but a useless waste of time," stormed Verity, angrily brandishing her fork. "It's a pity someone from the Council Offices can't be chased by the wretched bull. It might make them move a bit more quickly then."

"They would have to move if they were being chased by Ford's black Friesian," laughed Hallam

Rand, the humour of the situation suddenly striking him. "I wouldn't give much for the chances of the chap I saw this morning, in such circumstances. He was as round as a ball," he grinned. "Though the exercise might be beneficial if he managed to get away with it."

"It's hardly a waste of time, Vee, even if Hal didn't get very far," pointed out her father. "It's all progress, even if it is slow. It won't help by us getting het up about it."

"But they're so slow!"

"It's a County law we're trying to alter, and it takes time."

"It's a potential loss of life you're trying to prevent," cried Rob vehemently, as vexed as Verity. "Can't they see that, stuck in their safe little offices?"

"I think we ought to send the girls next time, Bill. They would make better ambassadors for our cause," smiled the vet, in no way put out.

"They would certainly make better looking ones," laughed the farmer.

"I agree." Hal Rand smiled at Verity. "How about it, Vee? Are you willing to put on a sandwich board, and start parading for us?"

Automatically he used the childhood diminutive, and the girl smiled back at him warmly.

"I would be more inclined to wield my sandwich board as a knobkerrie," she laughed, and the vet laughed with her, his grey eyes merry and carefree, the shutters of reserve rolled back from his face, and his normally aloof expression chased away by sheer, boyish fun.

"He looks a different person," thought Rob, fascinated. "And at least ten years younger."

It was only with Verity that he seemed to let the barriers of reserve drop, and be his real self. They were a handsome couple, the platinum-haired girl and the black-haired man, thought Rob, not for the first time. Verity had taken her coffee, and disdaining a chair, curled up on the rug beside Hallam Rand's chair, using his knee as a backrest. Red gave her a look of disgust, obviously put out at being usurped from what he regarded as his own reserved place, and seeing that Verity did not intend to give way to him, he padded across to Rob, circled the spot by her feet two or three times, and slumped down with a sigh of content. She reached down a sympathetic finger and fondled his ear, and he responded with a length of rough pink tongue. She tried to reach down to rub his neck, a favourite spot just underneath his collar, but her arm was not long enough, she was too deep into the armchair, so she wriggled forward the better to reach him. Bill Wade came across, and put his coffee down on a nearby table.

"Here, tuck these cushions behind your back. You're lost in that big chair," he told her.

He reached down and caught her arm, easing her forward the better to thrust the cushions behind her. His hand touched the bruise, hidden beneath her blouse sleeve, and Rob gave an involuntary gasp and turned white.

"Oh!"

At the first sound, the setter rose to his feet in one fluid movement and faced Bill Wade menacingly, a snarled warning curling his lips back from his teeth. The farmer turned a shocked face to Rob.

"I'm sorry, Rob. I didn't think I'd grabbed you that hard."

"No. No, you didn't." Rob spoke hastily, as taken aback by the setter's reaction as the farmer. "It's all right, really," she assured him, for he still looked concerned. "I just—bumped my arm in that spot. You happened to touch the bruise, that's all," she explained, her hands reaching out to the still bristling dog. "It's all right, Red," she soothed him, her fingers smoothing his hackles, desperately wishing he would quiet, for the eyes of the whole room were on him, and as a consequence on her. She waited until the setter lay down again, muzzle on paws, though with his eyes still fixed on Bill Wade as if warning him not to come near. With one hand restrainingly on the dog's head, Rob reached back with the other and tucked the cushions behind her in the chair.

"That's a lot comfier. Thank you very much." She smiled at the farmer, hoping to divert his attention, but his surprise was too evident.

"It's absolutely incredible," gasped Verity, sitting bolt upright on the rug. "Red has simply never acknowledged anyone's existence before, except Hal's. You must have bewitched him, or something," she accused Rob.

"It must be the colour of her hair," teased the farmer. "It's practically the same as Red's."

"How did you bruise your arm, Rob? Is it much?" Verity's mother sounded concerned.

"Oh no, really." Rob wished they would forget her bruise, and talk about something else. "It just happens to be a fresh one, that's all."

"What did you do, fall out of your car again?" quipped her husband.

"I . . ." She threw a desperate glance towards Rand, and he came easily to her rescue.

"I beat her," he announced calmly, reaching for his pipe, and seemingly unaware of the startled glances of his three guests. Verity stared at him as if she was seeing him for the first time, and Rob's heart sank. "Oh dear," she thought, "if only he'd let me have my dinner with Martha."

"I hope you chastised her thoroughly." The farmer recovered first. "I don't believe in all this Women's Lib myself. A hiding twice a week. . . . But as you see, I'm outnumbered," he gestured towards his women-folk.

Hallam Rand tossed his tobacco pouch across to the farmer to help himself, and apologised for his pet's behaviour.

"Sorry about that, Bill. No, I'm not," he corrected himself immediately. "I'm sorry it had to be you he went for," he told the farmer, "but at least I know that he'll offer some protection to Rob when she's out on rounds. I've told her she's to take Red with her whenever she has to go out." He dropped his bombshell calmly, stuffing his pipe until he had it packed to his satisfaction. He lit a taper and held it to the tobacco, and a whiff of aromatic smoke blew across the room. Rob liked the smell of his tobacco. It was different from her father's, lighter and sweeter, but nice. She sniffed appreciatively, and glanced at the faces around her. They were all looking at their host, each of them registering various degrees of shock, and she felt a chuckle start inside her.

Mrs Wade looked at the vet with a puzzled crease across her forehead, for all the world as if she was wondering whether he was about to start a temperature. Bill Wade simply stared, disbelief large in his eyes, the vet's tobacco pouch unopened in one hand, and his pipe unheeded in the other. It was if he was about to start conducting a band, thought Rob, and bit back a smile. Verity's blue eyes were round. She looked from her human backrest to the dog, and back again, as if she did not believe the evidence of her own ears. Red stirred under Rob's hand, and she tensed, wondering what he was going to do. He got to his feet, but his eyes were mild, and looked in the direction of the window, out towards the mill wheel.

"What's he listening for?"

Verity watched him intently, but over the rumble of the wheel they could hear nothing, and the garden seemed empty of movement.

"Probably a cat," suggested her father.

"If it had been, Red would be gone by now, and so would the cat," laughed the vet. "No, he's heard something that we can't—ah, there it is!"

The dog whined, and looked at his master, and over the rumble of the wheel came a heavier sound, lowering from the heat-hazed sky.

"It's all right, Red. Lie down. It's only thunder."

Rob stroked him, her hands gentling the long, loose curls of his coat, feeling the vibration of a tremble as the thunder came again. She watched for lightning, but none came.

"That storm has been hanging about for the past twenty-four hours," said the farmer unhappily, glancing up at the sky with a typical countryman's 'one eye on the ground and one in the air' look.

"Well, I hope it doesn't break all over the garden fête on Saturday," his daughter retorted with some asperity. "After all that work we've put in, it will be a criminal shame if it's a washout."

"Well, it's no use grumbling to me," laughed her father. "I'm not responsible for the weather. But I wish it would either break or clear off," he continued uneasily. "The air is getting heavy, and it's making the animals restless."

"Any signs of trouble?" Hallam Rand's interest was immediate, and professional.

"Not as yet," replied Bill Wade, stuffing his pipe in turn. "But I hate these electric storms. With one of them hanging overhead it puts the cattle on edge, and I never feel really easy until it's cleared," he confessed. "The animals won't settle, and you can't. They hate storms."

"They're not the only ones," Verity put in. "They give me the jitters, too. When I think of that elm tree

last year. . . . The lightning just cleaved it in two."
Her hands parted the air in an expressive gesture, and
she grimaced in Rob's direction. "I was standing under
it, sheltering from the rain, about a quarter of an hour
before it was struck."

"Then you should have had more sense," her father
retorted sharply. "Of all the daft things to do, when
there's a storm about!"

"It would have put a parting in your hair if you'd
stayed there." Hallam Rand ruffled the straight, flaxen
strands against his knee. They floated about his slim,
brown fingers like threads of ivory silk, and settled
back into place about Verity's head, pulled by their
own weight into a shining smoothness as if they had
never been disturbed. "Never mind about the thunder,
concentrate on what you're going to wear for the
dance on Saturday night, and you'll forget about the
weather."

His voice was soft and affectionate, and he left his
hand resting lightly on her head. Verity smiled across
at Rob.

"What are you going to put on, Rob?"

"What about that green dress and sandals we saw
you in the other evening?" suggested her mother.
"With your pretty hair. . . ."

"Oh no, it's got no sleeves in it," said Rob, then
stopped and bit her lip. She had told them she had
bruised her arm, but she was conscious herself that the
bruises were obvious fingermarks, and she knew that if
she went in a sleeveless dress they were bound to cause
comment. She did not want to embarrass either herself

or her employer by having to answer questions on that score.

"It won't be cold, not at the annual village hop," laughed the farmer. "If the crowd we get in the village hall is anything to go by, you'll be glad of something with no sleeves before the night is out. The men usually end up with their jackets off," he assured her.

He reached down and pulled his wife gently to her feet, and at the same time gave Verity's hair a tug.

"Come on, you two girls," he winked at Rob. "Home, before the storm starts. It takes all the curl out of my hair," he complained plaintively, and the others laughed.

They were still smiling when they said goodbye at the front doorstep. Rob held back in the hall, not wishing to push herself, sure the vet would want to say goodnight to Verity in private, but he gave her no chance to disappear into the kitchen to Martha as she intended. He cupped his hand round her elbow in a way that was rapidly becoming a habit when he wanted to make sure that she did not escape him, and took her with him on to the outside step.

He shook hands with Bill Wade and kissed Mrs Wade and Verity lightly on the cheek before seeing them into their car, then came back and stood beside Rob on the step, and together they watched the tail light disappear down the street on its way back to Wade Hollow.

As they turned to go indoors together, the man's eyes searched the sky, anxiously seeking some signs of rain bearing cloud. The last of the sunlight had gone, leaving the sky empty of warmth, grey with the gathering darkness, and with only the rumble of thunder, distant but ominous, and the thickening, electric air, to warn them of the impending storm.

CHAPTER NINE

"YOU'VE won, Miss Fenton! You've won!"

Jimmy jumped up and down with excitement, landing on the grass and Rob's toes with complete impartiality. Rob removed her feet to a safer distance, and smiled at the woman behind the hoopla stall.

"I didn't know I was such a straight shot!" She accepted her prize—a ping-pong ball on which some village artist had painted a gay little face—and reached down for Jimmy's hand. "Come on, let's go and cool down with a glass of lemonade or something."

"And a bun." The two went together in Jimmy's young mind, and at the mention of food Sam, hitherto a hot and not very interested observer of the antics of human beings at church fêtes, rose shaggily and set off at once in the right direction.

"He knows the way," explained his young master earnestly. "I had to bribe him before he'd go in the ring for the dog show."

Rob smothered a smile.

"How did he get on?" she asked cautiously.

"Oh, Miss Wilberforce won—at least, her dogs did," qualified Jimmy, "but of course there were two of them. Whisky and Soda, you know," as if that explained everything. "I think Mr Rand might have given it to Sam, otherwise. He said he was a—a—beeyootiful example of his breed," he remembered, with a rush of pride.

"And so he is." Verity dropped on to the grass beside them with a gasp of relief. "Whew! I'm so hot. Thank goodness for lemonade." She took a long drink through her straw then, cooled off, she looked at the child. "You went off without your prize, Jimmy."

"What prize? There wasn't. . . ."

"There was. One for special breeds," said a deep voice above them. "And that was Sam." Hallam Rand collapsed on to the turf beside Verity, and regarded the lad with a serious face. "You'd better take it now. I had to collect it for you because you'd gone."

He held out a gaily wrapped package, and the little boy's face lit up. He took it eagerly, and undid the wrapping with hasty fingers.

"Ooh, it's a collar! Oh! It's pink." He eyed it doubtfully.

"Hmm, yes." The donor eyed the offending colour with some dismay. "I didn't think when I bo . . ." He stopped abruptly and moved his shin ruefully out of reach of Verity's toe. "Oh well, never mind. A bit of saddle soap will bring it up a nice nut brown. I'll sort some out for you when I get back to the surgery, and let you have it the next time I pass the Martyr's Arms," he promised.

"Thanks, Mr Rand." Jimmy raised a grateful face, and spotted his father heading in their direction. "Dad, Sam won a prize after all. Isn't that great?"

Tom Grant strolled up and regarded the party on the grass.

"Won what? I thought there was only one prize for the dog show?"

A ferocious scowl appeared simultaneously on the faces of both Verity and the vet, and stopped him in mid-sentence. He looked down upon his son, and the mop of hair beside him that was busily demolishing more than its rightful share of Jimmy's bun, and smiled at the vet.

"Thanks, Hal."

The vet looked embarrassed.

"He's in a class of his own, is Sam."

"Why, that's just what Miss Fenton said," exclaimed Jimmy, delighted. "And Mr Rand is bringing me some soap," he went on, to his father. "For the collar, I mean," he qualified hurriedly, "to change its colour. Sam can't wear pink, can he, Dad?"

"From the look of both of you the soap is needed for more than the collar," retorted his father drily. "Collect your belongings, boy, it's time we went home. Opening time soon," he explained.

"But, Dad, the fête isn't finished yet!"

His father eyed him speculatively.

"Well, I suppose another half hour won't hurt,

providing you have no more ice creams. But come straight home afterwards," he warned the boy.

"He can stay with me if you like," offered Rob. "I'll see him back. And I promise not to feed him," she smiled, seeing Tom Grant relent.

"Very well, but just be good," the publican commanded his son, with the inbuilt distrust of every parent. "Don't let him be a nuisance to you, Rob."

"He can help me, as a matter of fact," replied Rob, and gained Jimmy's immediate interest. She held up the ping-pong ball. "I think I've seen the old lady I took the kitten to, somewhere about," she told him. "It would be nice if we could find her, and give her the ping-pong ball for the kitten to play with. I'm afraid it's too small for Sam," she apologised to Jimmy.

"Oh, he'd only eat it." Jimmy regarded his faithful follower with a complete lack of illusion. "He eats most things."

"A walking dustbin, in fact." Rob shook her head reprovingly. "Come on, let's go and find the old lady."

She stood up and brushed down her slacks. She did not want to make a third with Verity and her employer. The vet's off duty hours were scarce enough, without her playing gooseberry while he and Verity did have time together. She felt badly enough about the dance that evening as it was. If she had not been around, Rand would have taken Verity on his own, but as she was living in the same house, and Verity herself had mentioned it, he could hardly back out of taking her now. She held out her hand to the child, and he grasped her fingers with a sticky paw.

"Come on, Sam."

One end of the woolly bundle looked up. An energetic pink tongue appeared, and licked up the remains of the bun from around the grass where he had been lying, then when he had decided that there were definitely no more crumbs hidden under the short green blades, he heaved himself reluctantly to his feet and padded after them. Rob could hear him panting behind them with the enthusiasm of a small steam engine, and shortened her stride to let him catch up.

"You'll have to dock his rations, Jimmy. He's getting fat."

Jimmy regarded his property dubiously.

"That's what Mum said, but Dad said it was only his hair growing," he told her. "One of the days when there's time, we're going to have him properly clipped out, but we're busy at the Arms just now, with the summer visitors," he explained seriously.

Rob smiled. She had not seen all that many tourists in the village. There was sometimes an odd car or two, but mainly they were people who were just passing through, stopping for a break in their journey and a meal at the inn. Barshire had not the attraction of a Bard, like Warwickshire, to tempt sightseers within its environs, and it was rare for the population of the village to exceed its normal numbers, most of whom were gathered now among the stalls, looking for a bargain or a gossip as the mood took them.

Rob let Jimmy lead the way. She had only caught

a fleeting glimpse of the kitten's owner, and had no real idea whether or not she was still at the fête, so one direction was as good as another in which to look for her, and as her main object was to leave Verity and the vet on their own it did not particularly matter. She had promised not to feed Jimmy, and voluntarily extended that promise to include Sam, regarding his portly person with a professional shake of the head, but she felt at liberty to let the boy have a go at the hoopla, then went on to roll a penny, ring the bell— Jimmy's biceps were much too puny to get the hammer even half way up to its target, and Rob was much too hot to try—and finally spent all her remaining coppers on some wildly unsuccessful shots at the coconut shy. She had two balls left, and eyed the serenely untouched nut with something akin to despair.

"I wanted one to hang up in the garden for the birds," wailed Jimmy plaintively.

"Then you try. I miss every time."

She handed him one of the balls, and he looked at it doubtfully.

"I can't throw far enough."

He had thrown three already, and narrowly missed the stall minder with two of them. That good lady moved hastily out of the way.

"Let me try, and see if I can get one for you."

Jimmy and Rob turned to see the vet standing just behind them, watching their efforts with unconcealed amusement.

"Will you, Mr Rand?" Jimmy handed over his ball

eagerly. "I wanted that one, in the middle." He pointed to a large, round nut, with a top knot of frizzy fibre.

The vet smiled at Rob.

"Haven't you made contact, either? In my experience, you usually manage to!"

Rob's cheeks flamed. He still had not forgotten their first disastrous encounter, but he need not have brought it up now.

"I hope he misses!" she thought furiously, and instantly felt ashamed. Jimmy did so want the coconut. Hallam Rand drew back his arm, and threw. The ball flew through the air, there was a gasp from Jimmy, and then a disappointed "Oh, you missed!" He had, but only by a fraction of an inch. The nut rocked in its holder with the wind of the ball passing, and for one tense second Rob thought that it would fall, but it steadied and settled back safely. She felt guilty, as if her wish had transferred its bad influence to the vet's aim, and held out her last ball.

"Try this one."

The vet took it from her hand, his grey eyes on her face, still with the smile in them. Rob realised with a sense of shock how young he looked when he was relaxed. His afternoon with Verity had done him good. But where was Verity? She looked round, but there was no sign of the girl. She had probably been buttonholed by one of her numerous friends. The people at Wade Hollow were known to everyone in the neighbourhood, and seemed to be liked by them all, with the exception of Lewis Ford, the farmer at Norton End.

"You've hit it! You've hit it! Oh, isn't that great, Miss Fenton? I've got my coconut!"

Jimmy blissfully assumed that the nut would be his, and Hallam Rand looked at Rob, his expression a mute appeal for permission. She nodded, smiling, childishly relieved that her unkind wish had not come true, and laughed along with the vet when the stall-holder handed the little boy his coveted prize, and he wriggled in dismay as the stiff top fibres stuck through his thin tee-shirt.

"Here, hold it by the hair, like this, from the top."

The vet demonstrated, and Jimmy wrapped his small fingers round the top-knot, and carried it proudly.

"He looks a bit like a head-hunter," chuckled the vet, watching him strutting along in front of them, with a curious Sam trotting close in order to get near enough to have a sniff at the odd-looking thing swinging from his small master's hand. He lost interest when he decided that whatever it was, it was not food, and dropped behind them, following at his own, much slower pace.

A group of lively youngsters, in purloined sacks, suddenly erupted from one of the tents, and set off on an impromptu sack race of their own towards the lemonade stall. Rob and Hallam Rand were caught in their midst, hustled from all sides, and the laughing vet put his arm around her, steadying her against the onrush.

"They'd get there a lot quicker without the sacks," laughed Rob, watching the hopping crowd disappear with thirsty speed.

"Ah, but it's more fun going in a sack when you're that age. At least, it is if you've got someone else to play with." His voice was unconsciously wistful, and Rob looked up at him quickly, touched by the revelation of a vulnerable human being inside his usually reserved exterior.

"How lonely he must have been," she thought, with quick compassion. "He probably still is." But that was silly. How could he still be lonely, when he had Verity? The thought came unbidden, and something inside her flinched. The thought of the fair-haired girl from Wade Hollow made her conscious that Hal's arm was still about her, and she moved slightly, causing his hand to drop. He looked down at her quickly, and she felt him stiffen.

"Now I've annoyed him again," she thought. Everything she did seemed to have the same effect on him. She lifted her hand and brushed the errant curl from her forehead; it still would not stay up. "I must have it cut," she thought, "if I can find a good hairdresser." Maybe in Barhill, when she had got an hour free. Although there was so little time to go now until the end of the month that it would hardly be worth it. She might as well wait, and have it done at home while she was waiting for another post.

Suddenly the sun felt unbearably hot, and she wished the fête would end, and she could go back to Mill House, to the cool room overlooking the river, with the sound of the waterwheel a murmur in the background. An ache in her hand made her look down, and she realised that she had been gripping the little ping-pong ball tightly within her palm. The vet caught her glance, and spoke.

"Haven't you found the old lady yet?" His voice was cool, impersonal as when they were attending a patient together, the laughter gone from his eyes. He glanced about the crowd, thinning now that the races were done, and it was getting towards tea time. "It looks as if—yes, there she is, over there by the tent." He slid his hand under Rob's elbow, his greater height enabling him to see over the heads of the people about them, and steered her in the right direction.

"We've come to see how Jet is getting on," he stated, annexing the kitten's owner just as she was about to move off.

Delight flooded the old lady's face, and Rob felt a sudden, warm glow inside her because the vet had remembered the name they had given to the kitten. He listened patiently while the owner gave a blow-by-blow account of its doings since the day it had come into her care, and he gave no sign of impatience, but promised to come and see the kitten some time when he was passing, 'to keep an eye on it for you' as he put it. Instinctively Rob knew that he would keep his promise, and also that he would not charge the owner any fee. She knew that the bill she had made out in the surgery for her attention to the old lady's previous cat had never found its way to the post, and across the counterfoil, in the vet's firm, black handwriting, she had read the word 'Cancelled'. A crony of their companion's, a fellow member of her local Guild, eventually claimed her, and released them to go in search of Verity.

"She joined up with her parents," said the vet, "and they got buttonholed. You know how it is in these small communities, everyone knows everybody else."

"The Wades seem to have a lot of friends."

"They ought to," retorted her companion, "they've lived in Martyr's Green for long enough."

"Four hundred years at Wade Hollow." Unconsciously Rob echoed her own words on the first day that she had met Bill Wade. It must be good to have roots that went as deep as that. Her own family had been in Devon for generations, but not so long as the Wades had been at Wade Hollow. And soon the vet would join them. Like a graft on to an old tree, thought Rob, that thrust its own roots into the ancient stock until it became one with the whole, and indistinguishable except by the vigour of its growth that rejuvenated the life stream for the branches yet to grow.

Rob caught sight of Verity and her parents first. They were just coming out of the nearby tent, accompanied by another, youngish man. Verity was busily licking an ice cream cornet. She spun round at the sound of the vet's hail, and a blob of ice cream transferred itself to her chin. The vet slid his fingers into the pocket of her dress and fetched out her handkerchief.

"What on earth is the use of this?" He held up the

minute, lace-edged square incredulously, then dropped it back where it came from and shook out a large white one from his top pocket. "Hold still while I wipe your face." He busied himself with his task, making a thorough job of it. "You always were messy with ice cream."

Verity accepted his ministrations calmly, returning to her cornet unrepentant when he had finished.

"I still feel grubby," she complained. "If we're going to leave ourselves time to get ready for the dance tonight, we ought to be going soon. It must be nearly six o'clock."

Her father nodded, and turned to the fair-haired man who had come out of the tent with them.

"That's it then, Martin. I'll arrange to send the beasts over for next week's market, and leave the rest to you. Oh, I'm sorry, Rob," he apologised, turning to her, "you must think we're an ill-mannered lot. But you're so tiny, you were half hidden behind Hal," he smiled. "This is Rob Fenton, Martin," he introduced her to the young man. "Martin Bradley, our tame auctioneer."

Rob smiled and held out her hand, and found it clasped in a firm grip.

"So you're Hal's assistant? I've heard a lot about you."

He did not say what he had heard, or from whom, and Rob wondered which of her particular blunders had taken precedence.

"I think it's time we took young Jimmy home," butted in the vet, looking around. "Where on earth . . .

oh, there you are." He reached out a hand and seized Jimmy by the slack of his shirt, and the faithful Sam immediately did an about-turn from whatever errand he had been bound upon, and joined the group along with his master.

"I'll come and pick you up at about eight o'clock, Vee," continued Hallam Rand, "if that's all right?"

"Fine," replied Verity, licking the remains of her ice cream from her fingers. "I shall be a bit cleaner by then, I hope," she grimaced.

"We'll see you there, Martin?"

The fair-haired man nodded, smiled pleasantly at Rob, and turned away with Verity and her parents, heading for the car park. Rob noticed that he limped slightly as he walked.

The vet had left his Land Rover in the driveway of the vicarage for a quick getaway in case he was called out to an urgent case, and Rob and Jimmy and the panting Sam followed him in the opposite direction from the others. Within a few minutes, the boy was proudly displaying his coconut to his parents, and Rob and the vet were on their way back to Mill House, and the quiet rooms that she had been longing for for the past hour.

The air seemed cooler by the water, and by the time she had bathed and changed she found she was looking forward to the dance. Verity had inferred that there would be a crowd of people they knew, so she might not after all be solely dependent on the vet as an escort. She found it distasteful to have to share another girl's escort, but after all, she consoled herself, it was Verity who had suggested the idea in the first place. The vet had been more or less pushed into it. A mischievous quirk turned up the corners of her lips, and lit up the amber depths of her eyes, and she slipped her clothes over her head, surprised to find her spirits lighter than they had been for some days. The fan-pleated skirt of her coffee-coloured dress just hid her knees, its three-quarter sleeves and tight, high-necked bodice giving it a demure look that suited her. She buckled a slender gold belt about her waist, matching the colour of her slippers, and on an impulse she reached across to the vase of roses that Martha had put on her dressing table, and snapped off a tight, cream-coloured bud. She tucked it firmly into the thick waves of her hair, where it nestled against her curls, the soft, pale petals complementing the creamy pallor of her skin. The sleeves of her dress felt over-warm in the thundery air, but it was the only one she had with her that was suitable, and would at the same time cover the bruise on her arm.

She picked up her evening bag and a featherlight Chinese silk stole, then ran downstairs, anxious not to keep the vet waiting. He had said they would be at Wade Hollow by about eight, and it was half past seven now. He came out of the study door as she reached the bottom stair, his face veiled in the shadow of the darkened room behind him. His dark hair was brushed back in an attempt to control the deep waves that he seemed to dislike so much. "He has the same trouble as me," thought Rob, with an inward smile, and came towards him feeling suddenly shy. The magpie colouring of evening clothes suited his lithe slimness, making him look, if anything, taller than ever, and she wished her gold sandals had higher heels. She felt a bit like a schoolgirl, with her head not reaching up to his shoulder. Verity's reached past it, she was almost as tall as he was. They would have tall children, thought Rob, tall and straight like the chimneys of Wade Hollow.

Red padded forward, obviously expecting to come with them, and his master checked him with a quiet word.

"Not tonight, Red. I'm looking after her instead." He reached out and took Rob's arm, his eyes inscrutable as he glanced down at her slender form beside him, but he said nothing as he suited his stride to hers down the shallow front steps. Rob checked in surprise as she caught sight of the gleaming Lancia pulled up at the bottom. She had never given their mode of transport a thought. She was so used to the vet's Land Rover that she supposed she had automatically thought they would go in that.

"I couldn't take you in the Land Rover." Hallam Rand sounded shocked, divining her thoughts. "Not in a dress as pretty as that."

"I didn't know you had. . . ." Rob stopped, suddenly realising that it might sound rude.

"I don't take it out very often." The vet undid the passenger door and helped her in, bending down to tuck her dress safely out of the way of the door, then he shut it on her and slipped into the seat beside her. The engine purred into life, indicative of a higher than usual horsepower underneath the long bonnet, and Rob snuggled back.

"This is what motoring should be." Her voice betrayed her enthusiasm, and her companion glanced down at her appreciatively.

"I've never had much time to take her out," he confessed, "but I intend to alter that now," implying that he had more time now that she was helping him. More time to spend with Verity. Rob made no comment, she was content to sit beside him and enjoy the unaccustomed luxury of the powerful car, and happily able to leave the driving to him. He was a superb driver, handling the huge machine with an easy mastery that drew her respect, and the ride was not nearly long enough for her. She said so when they pulled up in front of Wade Hollow, and he turned to her, obviously pleased.

"I'll take you for a longer spin in her," he promised impulsively, "as soon as we get a spare afternoon."

Rob looked up at him, startled, but the dusk of the car hid her surprise, and then they were in the hall of Wade Hollow, greeting Bill Wade and his wife, and Verity was running down the wide stairs to meet them. Her ballet-length, delphinium blue dress was a perfect match for her eyes, and the wide velvet band that held back her pale hair. Her silver fairness gave her an almost ethereal look against the dark panelling of the walls, and Rob's throat constricted.

"She looks more like a painting than a person," she thought, and suddenly felt her own dress to be dowdy and colourless in comparison. She was silent as they went back to the car, but the others did not seem to notice. Verity chattered to the vet, and he responded in the warm, amused tone that he only seemed to use when he was with her. Rob had occupied the seat beside him on the way, but now Verity slid into it with an automatic ease that spoke of habit, and Rob reached out for the handle of the back door. It was locked, and the vet opened it for her, tucking her in with the same care that he had used when they started from Mill House. She thanked him quietly, and he gave a keen look in her direction, hesitated, then shut the door and got into the driving seat beside Verity without saying anything. Rob felt glad when they arrived at the village hall and found a crowd of people of about their own age waiting for them.

"You're late," they were accused, "you're the last to get here."

"Blame the girls for titivating," the vet basely denied responsibility, and claimed Verity for the first dance. It was a waltz, and Martin Bradley bowed his request to Rob. The band was surprisingly good. "Local talent," explained the auctioneer, "but they're very keen. They've won quite a name for themselves hereabouts."

A quickstep followed, and Martin Bradley confessed his inadequacy and led her back to their table. Verity and Hallam Rand joined them, and the two men went off in search of refreshments, for it was hot in the hall. As they moved away the young auctioneer's limp was noticeable, and Verity caught Rob's glance.

"Some cattle ran amok in the market," she explained quietly. "Martin tried to stop them, and got pretty badly trampled. It left him with one leg slightly shorter than the other, and it tips his balance a bit if he tries anything faster than a waltz."

That explained why he had opted out of the quick-step.

"What caused them to stampede?"

"Thundery weather. Weather like this," said the other. "It seems to bring out all the stinging, biting insects that ever lived, and it drives the animals mad. It only needs some slight incident for them to run wild. I wish it would rain," she added, a crease forming between her eyes.

"There speaks a farmer's daughter!"

Martin Bradley returned with lemonade, and a teasing look in Verity's direction.

"We were wishing it would get cooler," she countered with a smile, accepting her drink, her feet tapping to the music as the band started up a slow foxtrot. Hallam Rand stood up and smiled at Rob, claiming the dance. To her surprise she found that he was no mean performer on the floor. Instinctively tucking herself close under his arm, she gave herself up to the music. She was a born dancer, light and supple in her movements, and the two of them circled the room without speaking, lost in the rhythm. The music stopped, and for a second they stayed close where their steps had taken them, then Rob sighed and relaxed. She dropped her arms, but Hal kept her hand in his.

"There might be a repeat," he hoped.

The music started again, but this time it was a

waltz. Without speaking Hal gathered Rob back into his arms, and once more they circled the floor. Her pleated skirts swung as they spun, allowing her free movement, and his grasp on her tightened as they pirouetted. She adjusted herself automatically in his arms, matching her steps to his until the two of them were one fluid movement, motivated by the soft, insistent beat of the music. Her head rested in the hollow below the vet's shoulder, and the faint perfume from the rose in her hair made an aura of sweetness about them as they spun. Time ceased to exist, there was nothing except the music, and the man's firm arms about her, and it was with an effort that Rob shook herself back to reality when the last notes faded into silence, and she found herself back at their table, with Martin Bradley handing her her neglected drink.

"Cool off," he advised her smilingly. "If it keeps as hot as this we shall empty the cellars at the Martyr's Arms!"

"Isn't it a lovely old place?" Rob's voice was enthusiastic. "I went there the other day."

"What, to the pub?" The auctioneer raised surprised eyebrows.

"Only to the living quarters," qualified Rob, her colour rising. "I had tea with Mr and Mrs Grant, and Jimmy."

"Here's another one who's been there, but he hasn't been drinking tea." Martin Bradley looked towards the door, and his voice was a wary murmur. He held out his hand to Verity. "We seem to be in his line of approach. Shall we take the floor?" The dance was a waltz, and he whirled Verity away to the other side of the big hall.

"Let's do the same." Hallam Rand held out his hand, and Rob took it, glad to be dancing with him again. Their steps seemed to be a perfect match, despite the disparity in their height, and she enjoyed dancing with a good partner.

The M.C.'s voice announced a tag dance, and a lot of confusion and laughter ensued as people changed partners, but no one tagged Rob and the vet and they continued until they got near the door. There, a heavy hand dropped on Rob's shoulder, and she turned, smiling, to partner her 'tag'. Instantly the smile froze on her lips, and she shrank back into the shelter of Hallam Rand's arms. The man who had tagged her was Lewis Ford, and it was obvious that he was tipsy, and looking for trouble. That must have been what Martin Bradley meant when he took Verity off, she thought with dismay.

Hallam Rand held her close, with his arm about her waist, and faced the Norton End farmer squarely.

"This tag is not allowed."

Either Lewis Ford did not hear him, or he felt inclined to argue. He swayed towards them truculently, whisky fumes preceding him in a wave, and grabbed at Rob's wrist.

"Let her go!"

Hallam Rand's voice was vibrant, rigidly controlled, but the man in front of him was too tipsy to recognise the danger.

"I got a right. It's a tag, ain't it?"

He reached out his other hand, and quick as lightning Hallam Rand reacted. Rob did not even see him move. The vet's arm rose, the farmer gave a convulsive gasp and released her, and stumbled back nursing his wrist, a look of sullen anger on his swarthy face.

The dancers stopped, but the band, unable to see the cause of the fuss, played on uncertainly, eventually coming to a ragged halt, and there was silence in the hall except for the shuffle of feet, and an occasional voice asking what had happened. Through the silence came a rumble of thunder. It sounded close, as if the storm was near to breaking.

"Here's Alf Dodd."

The policeman's rubicund face appeared through the crowd, making its way towards them.

"I thought you might be making for here." The representative of the law sighed resignedly, and grasped Lewis Ford in an authoritative grip. "Come along, you! Sorry if he's been a nuisance to you and your lady, Mr Rand," he apologised. "He does seem to take a tilt at you whenever he gets in this condition. If he was sober, he'd know better," he added, eyeing the vet's broad shoulders with respect.

"It's because of your campaign about his bull, I suppose?"

Rob danced automatically, the lightness gone from her feet.

"Yes, he never misses an opportunity to be unpleasant if he can help it. I'm only sorry that some of it has rubbed off on you, especially on your night out."

The vet looked concerned, and Rob smiled at him

brightly, assuring him that it did not matter. But while she might deceive him, she could not deceive herself, and her feet dragged through the subsequent dances, weighted by a sense of depression that she could not acount for, and a feeling of foreboding heightened by the increasingly loud rumbles of thunder from overhead, as if some great beast of prey stalked there, biding its time until it pounced on the parched earth quivering below.

CHAPTER TEN

THE last working week of Rob's month's trial began badly.

The night had been stickily hot, thunder and occasional flashes of lightning disturbing the stifling air, although still the sky remained relentlessly dry. Added to the queer restlessness that seemed of a sudden to possess her, Rob found sleep elusive, and what little she had was disturbed by troubled dreams.

The following morning she overslept, and reached the breakfast table still only half awake, and in no mood for conversation. The vet gave her a keen glance, wordlessly pushed the coffee pot within reach, and carried on reading his morning mail, leaving her to come to in her own good time.

He had been very quiet during the weekend, spending all of Sunday at home, and most of it stretched out on the lawn, with Red as usual by his side. Neither man nor dog seemed possessed of any desire to go out, and Rob wondered where Verity was, that he seemed content to remain at home during his only really free day of the week.

"Come and be lazy," he bade her, fixing a deck-chair for her next to his own. "You make me feel guilty, buzzing about in this heat."

Rob stopped wondering, and joined him, calmed in spite of herself by the peace of the garden, and the soothing murmur of the mill wheel, now turned much more slowly by a depleted stream, lowered by the long drought. Purposefully she pushed her depression aside, intent on enjoying what was left of her brief stay in her lovely surroundings.

She supposed that her two confrontations with the farmer from Norton End, added to the stormy start to her post as Hallam Rand's assistant, had combined to upset her normally calm approach to life, but despite her determination, the fear persisted that her employer might yet find these a reason for dispensing with her services, and taking on a male assistant. The fear caused a hurt of surprising strength, that dimmed the brightness of the sunshine, and she stirred restlessly in her chair, her hands going out automatically to tease the setter's silky curls.

"I shall miss him, too," she had thought miserably, dejection spoiling the peaceful afternoon, despite her determination.

She tackled her breakfast egg now without enthusiasm, unhappy at the thought of finding herself an-

154

other post, which she knew without thinking about she would not like. The morning surgery did little to help her depression. For once, there were not a lot of patients, but the thundery air seemed to make those they had more troublesome than usual, and by ten o'clock both Rob and the vet had received a dog bite each. At half past, someone rang and asked Hallam Rand if he would go and cope with a swarm of bees that had alighted on a house gable, much to the house-holder's distress. With an asperity unusual for him when he was dealing with a prospective client, the vet informed the caller that he was a veterinary sur-geon, not a bee-keeper, and gave Jane Wilberforce's telephone number as the only person he knew locally who might be able to offer assistance. They found out, later, that the bees did in fact belong to the Wilberforce sisters, and they were even then in hot pursuit of the swarm, Jane in the lead, followed by a voluble Hetty carrying veils and all the paraphernalia necessary to recapture their demoralising pets.

The telephone rang again, and Rob relaxed for a second as the vet answered it. She rubbed a hand wearily across her hot face, only half listening to the conversation.

"I'll send my assistant out. Yes, right away." He put the receiver down, and turned to Rob. "Just the thing to give you a break from the surgery. I can finish off what there is to do here now."

"Where to?"

Rob was already reaching for her bag, thankful for the chance of a run outside.

"Barhill Market. It seems there's been a set-to between a billygoat and a pig. There's not much damage done, from what I can gather, but the pig seems to have received a cut on its hindquarter, and the owner is a bit incensed, and insists on having a vet."

"I'll try not to be too long."

"Take the rest of the day off," suggested the vet. "There's nothing much doing here, and you haven't had a chance to look round Barhill since you came. Verity and her father are bound to be there, I know Bill Wade was sending some stock in today."

"I heard him mention it to Martin Bradley on Saturday," nodded Rob.

"They always have lunch at the Bar Arms, so you won't be without company," said Hal, and fleetingly Rob wondered if he was sending her out of his way, if he was impatient for the week to end, when she would be gone, and he could have Mill House to himself again. Himself and Verity.

She thrust the thought from her. It was useless to make herself more miserable than she already was. She backed Hoppy out of the garage and pointed the bonnet in the direction of Barhill. It was cool in the car, and she enjoyed the drive through the quiet lanes, despite their snakelike twists and turns. She had got used to these by now, as she had got used to the heavy foliage that arched over them. She no longer felt smothered, only—sheltered—yes, that was the word. Mill House gave her the same feeling, she realised with a sense of surprise. It had grown on her during the last month, and made the ache at the thought of leaving even harder to bear. She glanced gratefully at Red, curled up on the seat beside her. Mill House extending its shelter while she was on rounds, she thought with a smile. It was a nice, safe feeling. If only it need not be a transient one, as well!

Hoppy's seat was not so comfortable as that of the vet's Lancia, and Rob wondered if he would remember his promise and take her for a drive in it before the week was out. It would be a very pleasant experience, just for once to have a long ride in a large car, with a skilful driver.

When she reached Barhill it was crowded. The ancient market town took its once-weekly bustle of activity with great seriousness, and the narrow, cobbled streets were filled with folk from the remote districts around, the men intent on the stock market, and the women on the produce side, with their weekly chance of shopping, and an exchange of news with seldom seen contemporaries an added bonus to their visit.

Rob inched the Austin cautiously past a stone preaching cross, and tucked herself in behind a large, loaded cattle wagon, obviously heading for her own destination. She had no idea where the actual market was held, but her unwitting guide took her, via several tight turns through even narrower streets, to a wide space filled with stock pens, and the familiar milling, protesting jumble of livestock awaiting the attention of the auctioneer. She leaned out of her car window and enquired directions of a shirt-sleeved giant leaning against the door of an empty cattle truck.

"You the vet? Take your car on further up the yard then, miss, where the market staff park. You'll find the small stock in the pens yonder," he gestured away to his right. "Your wounded pig will be somewhere there," he smiled. "If you want help with the billy-goat, just shout," he added, eyeing Rob's bright curls with appreciation.

She laughed.

"I hope they've got him under control before I arrive," she replied feelingly, and ran her car into the small, reserved space indicated by the driver. She reached for her emergency kit, and Red slipped out of the car at her heels. Rob felt a momentary concern over his possible behaviour with the other animals, particularly the Border collies that slunk, one at the heels of each man, like badger shadows throughout the aisles of the market. But the setter had been brought up to this situation, and trained to ignore it, and he trotted docilely behind her, and the farm dogs, working animals all, knew better than to try conclusions with him during their working hours. They were as intent on the business of the day as were the men whose heels they shadowed, and Rob relaxed her vigil, content to go her way in the sure knowledge that Red would follow without supervision, a pace or two behind.

She ran her quarry to earth eventually in a corner pen, and found it rooting happily among a litter of straw, evidently far less disturbed than its owner over the fracas with the goat. The pig ignored her while she cleaned and dressed a small contusion, then turned to placate the farmer, who was audibly afraid of a decrease in its value.

"No harm done, just a slight abrasion," she consoled him.

"For two pins I'd sue!"

"Let it rest, Solomon." Martin Bradley came up behind them, and rescued Rob, who felt at a loss what to say. "I'll work a bit harder and see that you get a good price," he promised the farmer, who hesitated, then gave a grunt not unlike his property, thought Rob with a giggle she dared not give vent to, and stamped away in the direction of the Bar Arms. The auctioneer turned to Rob.

"I must be off as well, but Mr Wade and Verity are on the other side somewhere. I think Verity wanted some of Jane Wilberforce's honey, she usually brings some produce in."

"She won't get any this morning," denied Rob with a chuckle. "Jane Wilberforce is rescuing her bees from a house in the village. They swarmed a couple of hours ago. Someone rang Mr Rand and asked him to cope," she explained.

"It's no good anyone ringing Hal to cope with bees. He's scared to death of them," laughed the auctioneer unfeelingly.

"I don't believe it," defended Rob. "Why, he's had one dog bite already this morning, and that didn't seem to bother him."

"Ah, but dogs play fair. Bees come at you backwards," smiled the auctioneer, still amused. "Look." He pointed beyond the second row of pens. "There's

Verity, just past those crates of pullets." He raised his hand in a wave, and Verity looked up, her face bright as she recognised him. She waved back, then noticing Rob she beckoned her over.

"Why not have lunch with us?" invited Martin Bradley. "We always go to the Bar Arms, and if you're on your own——?"

"I'd love to," Rob accepted immediately. She did not feel like spending the rest of the day with her own thoughts. "That is, if you don't mind?" she asked Verity, minutes later, as they strolled side by side along the length of the stock pens.

"Join us by all means," welcomed Verity without hesitation, in her usually friendly manner. "I'm glad you've come anyway," she confided. "I've got some news to tell you. I've just got to tell somebody," she added with a rush of honesty, "or I think I shall burst!"

"Just follow Red, he knows the way." Bill Wade came up the steps of the Bar Arms behind them, and called out as he saw Rob hesitate in the face of two possible doors. "This is one of his usual haunts, he knows which table to make for."

He spoke no more than the truth. The setter padded his way into a low-ceilinged room until he came to a place set in a bow window overlooking the street. Here he halted and looked behind him, then satisfied that his human charges had followed him safely he slid underneath the dark oak refectory table, and curled up with a sigh, his duty done. Rob subsided on to the bench seat, and the dog shuffled until he was against her feet, then lay still, a silky warmth against her legs. She wondered what it was that Verity had to tell her. Whatever news she had, Rob surmised that it must be good. Somehow, Verity seemed to glow. Her eyes shone, and there was a brightness about her face as if she hugged some secret, inner happiness to herself. It made Rob curious to know what it was she had to tell, but it was no good asking now, for Martin Bradley limped up to the table and the talk became general. His quick eye noticed the marks of the dog bite on Rob's hand, and he commented on it.

"I thought you said it was Hal who had the bite?"

"I collected one, too," she replied ruefully, "in the surgery this morning."

"Don't tell me that Hal has run amok?"

Rob giggled, her spirits lifting under the light-hearted banter, and the meal that followed was a merry one. Verity was at her best, bubbling with fun, her face vivid with that curious inner light.

A waiter appeared, and Rob felt Red stir and get up. She spoke to him, but the man smiled and shook his head, bidding her to wait. Bending low, he placed a large dish in a corner of the bow window, and the setter slid out from under the table and homed to it with the surety of long custom. She glanced at Bill Wade, questioning.

"Leave him alone," said the farmer. "He always has his dinner with us. They keep an old plate for him here, and he looks forward to the treat as much as we do."

The setter fed neatly, spilling nothing, as fastidious

as a cat with his eating, and Rob smiled a 'thank you' at the waiter. Their own lunch over, the men began a friendly wrangle over the bill, each insisting that he wanted to pay.

"Oh, no," protested Rob, flushing, "I couldn't possibly let you. I only came out here on a job."

"And stayed to have lunch with us," replied Bill Wade firmly. "No, it's no use grumbling," he stifled Rob's protests. "Your lunch is on me. And yours," he told the younger man.

Martin Bradley rose regretfully.

"I've got to go back to work," he mourned. "What are you two girls going to do?" He sounded wistful.

"I thought of having a look round Barhill while I'm here," said Rob. "Mr Rand said I could take the afternoon off."

"Good! Then I'll come with you." Verity annexed her eagerly. "I've got to do some shopping, and then we can have a nice long talk on our own."

"That disposes of us, from the sound of it," remarked her father with a smile.

"I thought you had to go to the Council offices?"

"So I have. I'll walk with you as far as there. The Council House is in the middle of the shopping centre," the farmer explained to Rob as she followed him out, Red padding at her heels. Martin Bradley and Verity followed them, and the auctioneer stopped at the turning back to the market. The farmer and Rob called their goodbyes across a pavement full of hurrying heads, and strolled on, Red pacing like a dark shadow at their heels. Rob turned her head once, to make sure that he was still there, and she hung back, glancing over the heads of the crowd.

"What's the matter?" asked the farmer. "Have you lost the dog?"

"No, Red is here, but we seem to have become separated from Verity."

"She'll catch us up," said her father cheerfully. "Come on, it's no use trying to find her in this crush. We'll wait for her by the steps of the Council House."

It seemed a sensible suggestion, with the street full of the hurrying market crowds, and Rob followed her companion closely, careful not to lose sight of him, too. Verity caught them up, looking flushed and breathless, just as they reached a quiet corner beside the steps leading up to the imposing-looking public building.

"Good luck!" called Rob, as Bill Wade started to mount. "I hope you have more success this time."

The farmer lifted his hand with a slightly resigned gesture, and carried on climbing, and Verity caught at Rob's arm.

"Come on, let's go and do our shopping, then we can have a stroll along by the river where it's quiet. Red hates getting his feet trodden on in the crowds, don't you, old boy?"

"It sounds as if Verity and Hallam Rand do this regularly," thought Rob. Perhaps it was a weekly ritual, and she had come in his stead today. The others had shown no signs of resenting the fact that she had usurped her employer's place, even Verity was still openly friendly, but just the same Rob felt an interloper, and depression tugged at her again.

The other girl did not seem to notice her drop in spirits, for which Rob was thankful. The crowded pavements helped, since they prevented the two girls from talking straight away, and after a small amount of shopping Verity led the way down a narrow, steeply sloping side street away from the crush. Evidently Red knew the way here, too. He trotted on in front, running thankfully along the uncluttered cobbles, stopping now and then to shake himself vigorously as if to rid his silky body of the feel of others pressing against him. The street dropped sharply, and Rob felt glad of her rubber-soled slip-ons that gave her a firm grip on the smooth stones. With a twist that resembled one of the lanes beyond the town, the street ended suddenly, and Rob gave a gasp of delight.

"How lovely!"

Through an ancient archway, a cool vista of trees and grass stretched ahead of them, ending in the gleam of water about a hundred feet away, and Red quickened his pace eagerly.

"Yes, isn't it? The Council did one sensible thing here, at any rate," replied Verity, "they turned the river banks into a park, and most people head this way for a breather at some time during market day."

There were not many people there now, and Rob commented on the fact.

"There's still the produce market to come," Verity told her. "And the smaller stuff still has to be auctioned. They get the bigger animals out of the way first, it makes more room, and they cán concentrate on the odds and ends and the poultry when they're gone. This place won't fill up until about mid-afternoon, and by that time we shall be on our way home."

Now that she had the opportunity to talk, Verity seemed curiously reluctant to do so, and Rob did not press her. If Verity wanted to confide her good news, whatever it was, that was up to her, but if she had changed her mind Rob did not feel that she had known her for long enough to force her confidence. They strolled along in the cool of the trees, the grass soft under their feet after the hard roundness of the cobbles in the town. Some friendly ducks came to the bank, and they raided Verity's shopping bag for biscuits to feed them with, giving some to Red at the same time to appease his jealous whimper. Rob rubbed his muzzle affectionately.

"If I feed you with titbits and make you fat, your boss will be palming me off with that bull terrier, and finding you an engagement elsewhere." She did not say that the dog's duties would soon be over anyway. That was between herself and the vet, though doubtless Verity knew of her imminent departure as well as she did. The other girl made no comment. She stood gazing dreamily out across the river, a slight smile curving her lips, lost in a world of her own of which her companion had no part.

Seeing that the titbits were gone, Red wriggled free and pushed past her, intent on exploring every nook and cranny of the interesting bank while he had the opportunity. The feel of him brushing against her legs brought her back to earth, and she turned to Rob, her smile broadening.

"That's what my good news consists of," she said softly. "An engagement."

"But I thought. . . ." Rob had thought that she was already engaged, although she realised now that she had never noticed a ring on Verity's finger.

"Oh, the family have known for ages, of course. Mother told you, I suppose?"

Rob nodded, mutely, and she went on happily.

"It isn't official yet, we've been waiting for the ring. I've had to have it made smaller to fit me, and the jeweller who's doing it has been abroad on holiday. That's why we've had to wait to announce it." She smiled in a conspiratorial fashion at Rob. "The ring will be ready this weekend, and we're going to announce it then. So don't say anything, will you, Rob? Just keep it a secret until Saturday, and then the whole wide world can know."

She spread her arms to include the park, and the ducks flew away, quacking in alarm, with Red in enthusiastic pursuit along the bank. The dark blue eyes laughed into Rob's, alight with the glow that had made her wonder at lunchtime.

"Oh, Rob, I'm so happy! I simply couldn't wait for it to be announced," she cried. "I just had to tell someone."

CHAPTER ELEVEN

"I WONDER if I ought to congratulate him?"

Rob looked at Hallam Rand over her cup of supper coffee. She had promised Verity not to say anything to anyone, but did that include Verity's fiancé-to-be as well? she wondered. He seemed calm enough, in all conscience, she thought, unlike the girl who was to be his bride. She was excited enough for the two of them.

The old church at Martyr's Green would make a lovely setting for a wedding, Rob thought wistfully, and Verity a lovely bride. White would suit her gentian blue eyes and silver fairness, and her tall, slender, model-like figure would carry off an ankle-length dress and train to perfection. With the handsome, dark-haired Hallam at her side they would make a fine couple.

She took a mouthful of coffee, and found she had difficulty in swallowing it. Somehow she had no appetite for her supper tonight, despite the fact that she had been hard at work for the better part of the day. She wondered if Hallam Rand would give her a reprieve, and ask her to stay and look after the practice while he was away on his honeymoon. Someone would have to, and she at least knew the ropes by now, and most of the regular patients. She had no illusions about her position when the newly married couple returned to Mill House afterwards. Verity would not want another girl of her own age living in the same house as herself and her husband, friendly though she seemed at the moment. Martha would come into a different category, of course, but if anything else was needed, this would certainly set the seal on Rob's departure from her post as the vet's assistant. Her fingers stopped their automatic smoothing of the setter's ears, and she suddenly became aware that Hallam Rand was speaking to her.

"Another coffee, Rob? Oh, you haven't finished that one yet."

There was a half amused smile on his face, and she realised that he had probably spoken to her for the fourth time. She returned to earth with a bump, quickly swallowed the rest of her cupful, and held it out for a refill, that she knew she would have as much difficulty in drinking as the first one. She did not want it, but she did not want to cause comment by her refusal, either. Her companion knew how much she liked coffee, and that she always had two cups, three if there was enough going. His hand reached out, slender and bronzed, and returned her filled cup, and she looked up to thank him.

Their glances met, and his grey eyes, gazing back into hers, held a sudden warmth and—could it be— a question in their cool depths? A question that brought to life another question, startling in its clarity, within the hopeless turmoil of her own mind. And it was one to which, lost in that cool grey stare, she found a devastating answer.

She loved Hallam Rand.

The rest of that evening was never very clear afterwards, in Rob's mind. Somehow she finished her coffee. Somehow she made small talk out of the day's doings, told him of the result of her visit to the market place, and that she and Verity had shopped together in Barhill—he would think it strange if she did not mention it, but she carefully steered away from repeating any conversation that they had had, in case she inadvertently betrayed Verity's confidence.

The vet responded, but he seemed half-hearted, as if his mind was elsewhere. He was probably thinking of Saturday, surmised Rob, and wondering if the ring would be ready as the jeweller had promised.

After what seemed an age, the clock struck eleven and she thankfully made her escape upstairs, to the blessed relief of her own room, and privacy. But if she could shut herself in her room, she could not shut her thoughts out. They ran round and round in her head like caged mice round an exercise wheel, on and on until she rammed desperate hands against her ears, trying to shut out the words that only echoed inside her own mind, until at last, bewildered and exhausted, she watched the dawn light filter through the curtains, and heard the first birds give sleepy twitters from the eaves outside her window. As the light grew stronger she fell into a troubled doze, her bed a tumbled litter of covers, and the persistent refrain from the mill wheel drumming endlessly through her mind.

He belongs to Verity. He belongs to Verity. He belongs. . . .

The week passed in a daze. Thunder clouds built up in great, massing heads, and the electrified air, hot and still, pressed against the earth until the tension became almost unbearable. Human tempers frayed, and among the animal population frequent fights broke out, with a resultant heavier workload during the daily surgery. Perversely, Rob felt glad of the extra burden. The sheer concentration that was necessary, as well as the constant fight against the clock, kept her mind and hands occupied, and although at first it was torture for her to work side by side with the vet, as the hours passed she hugged to herself the bitter-sweet pain of sharing that soon, she knew, must come to an end. For she had come to a decision. Whether Hallam asked her to stay or not, she would have to go, for her own sake as well as for Verity's. The end of her 'approval' time would give her the opportunity to leave the job without too many questions being asked, and without hard feelings. She could make the isolation of Martyr's Green her excuse, as it seemed that other assistants who had come to Mill House had done before her, and she could—yes—run away and hide herself, she admitted, in the anonymity she longed for. The bruises that Lewis Ford had made on her arm were as nothing to those that Hallam Rand had, however unwittingly, made on her heart, and her very being felt one huge ache that nothing in the surgery drugs cupboard could possibly hope to cure.

Martha became vocally concerned about her lack of appetite and white-faced dejection, and Rob made the excuse that she found the heat trying. Hallam gave her a keen glance when she came down to breakfast on the Saturday morning, and for the third day running refused anything but a slice of toast, which she nibbled without appetite and left on her plate.

"I've got to go into Barhill this morning," he told her. "Why not give yourself the morning off, there's no surgery today. If you want something to do, there's the saddle soap I promised young Jimmy, you could take that to him and stop over for a chat at the Martyr's Arms." He knew that she and Sue Grant had made friends, and that she was a welcome visitor at the village inn.

"He's going into Barhill for the ring," thought Rob wretchedly. Verity had said that it would be ready on Saturday. Aloud, she asked the whereabouts of the saddle soap, glad of an excuse to quit the table, and as soon as she had searched it out from the surgery cupboard she took it up to her room and lingered there, waiting for the vet to go. She did not want him to offer her a lift into the village, the risk of being in the close proximity of the Land Rover with him would be too painful. To her tensed nerves he seemed longer than usual in getting ready to go out, and finally she heard him making a phone call which she knew instinctively must be to Wade Hollow. His crisp voice floated up the stairs.

"I'll see you in about an hour, then. By the bottom of the Council House steps? Yes, that will do. 'Bye!"

There was a sharp click as the receiver went down, and then footsteps, and the front door slammed to with a thud. Rob listened for the Land Rover engine to start up, and let the sound die away in the distance before she opened her door and came downstairs, the

171

saddle soap clutched in her hand. She reached the hall, numb with a pain that somehow she must learn to bear, and Martha appeared from the kitchen quarters. The elderly housekeeper looked at her searchingly, but she made no comment, merely asking her possible whereabouts in case there were any telephone calls.

"I don't want to disturb Mister Hal this morning if I can help it," she said, and Rob's heart twisted.

No, he would not want to be disturbed while he and Verity collected their ring. She held out the tin of saddle soap for Martha to see.

"I'm going to take this along for Jimmy Grant," she explained. "He was a bit put out by the colour of the dog collar that—that Mr Rand gave him at the fête last week."

Even saying his name hurt, thought Rob dully, feeling a faint surprise that she could still make normal conversation. She felt anything but normal, but the ache was all inside her, and she supposed it did not show on the outside.

"Well, there's no need to hurry back, Miss Rob. Lunch will be a bit late today, to give Mister Hal a chance to get back from Barhill," Martha said, and Rob looked at her, surprised into speech.

"I would have thought . . . oh, never mind."

She would have thought the vet would have stayed on in Barhill with Verity, perhaps given her lunch there, and then an afternoon out. Not simply come back to Mill House for lunch as if it were an ordinary day. But perhaps he was bringing Verity back? Or maybe they were coming back, and going out again for the afternoon and evening, maybe in the Lancia? Rob remembered that he had taken the Land Rover with him just now, she had recognised the note of its engine.

She bit her lip angrily, and put a firm check on her thoughts. She must not let them run wild like that, such a road led to disaster, and anyway it was none of her business how Verity and her fiancé celebrated their engagement—or did not celebrate it. That was entirely up to them.

She collected Hoppy from the garage, and somehow the familiar feel of the uneven stuffing in the driving seat was comforting. The Austin was not so luxurious as the Lancia, but it was friendly. Perhaps now she would never have that ride in the big car that Hallam Rand had so carelessly promised her; probably he had forgotten all about it by now, anyway.

Red gave a sharp bark, reminding her of her promise to take him with her, and she opened the passenger door and waited for him to jump in. He curled up on the seat beside her, and looked at her questioningly, as if he sensed the disturbance in her mind.

"Your guard duty will soon be over." She rubbed his ears wistfully, and he flagged his tail in response, satisfied now that she had spoken to him. "Oh, Red, I feel so miserable!"

But by dint of a self-discipline she did not know that she possessed, none of her misery showed in her face when she parked the Austin on the green by the duckpond, waved with a false gaiety in response to the policeman's friendly greeting from the door of his cottage, and made her way towards the Martyr's Arms in search of Jimmy.

"He's across the fields at the ford, fishing as usual," said his father, pausing in the strenuous task of hauling casks of beer up from the cellar into the bar above.

"Then I'll go along and search him out," Rob decided. She did not want to go back to Mill House and spend the morning alone with her thoughts, and the walk along the river bank to the ford would be pleasant, as would Jimmy's company, she guessed. An hour spent with the child, in the uncomplicated pursuit of capturing minnows from the river, was just what she needed at the moment.

"I'll take the saddle soap along to show him," she told Tom Grant. "It's for the collar that he had last Saturday. Perhaps Sam has got it on?"

"Come back here for coffee," interrupted Sue Grant, appearing flushed from the kitchen. "I'll have the baking finished by then."

"Thanks, I will."

Rob stepped outside, out of the way of the busily occupied pair, and skirting the back of the hostelry she came to an ancient kissing gate let into an overgrown field hedge, that gave on to the footpath running along the river bank.

It was cooler by the water, though not much, and Red panted along behind Rob, both their footsteps flagging in the overpowering heat. If only the weather would break, thought Rob longingly as she looked at the brassy sky. If the storm came, it would clear the air and the heat afterwards would not then seem so bad. It never did at home by the sea, somehow the water always tempered the summers, no matter how hot they were, but here, inland, the earth absorbed the rays of the sun, and gave back the heat so that it came at you from both above and below. It shimmered now in iridescent waves across the flagging grass, causing Red to gaze at the water with longing eyes.

"You can go in when we get to the ford," promised Rob. She could see Jimmy in the distance, or at least Jimmy's hat. It was a new one, she noticed as she got nearer. They had never recovered the other from the river at Mill House. The wheel had taken it under, she recalled with a shudder.

Jimmy saw her coming and waved his fishing net, and Red quickened his pace. Soon he joined Sam in the water alongside the boy. Jimmy was bare footed as usual, his jam-jar in one hand showing tiny black figures scuttling round the sides.

"You've had a bit of luck." Rob indicated the jar.

"Oh yes, there are hundreds of them here. Come and look!"

Rob peered over the edge of the bank, and Jimmy beckoned her impatiently.

"You'll have to wade along here with me, you can't see the fish from the bank."

Well, why not? She had not paddled for ages. Swiftly Rob stripped off her stockings and shoes, and holding her skirts above her knees cautiously made her way to the middle of the ford to join the child.

The water felt cool and sweet, it was only just past her ankles, and for several yards on either side of the actual ford it ran shallow across smooth stones. An ideal place for the child to play.

"Come and look!"

Jimmy waded across and grabbed her hand, and she allowed herself to be pulled along the bank of stones to the centre of the river.

"There they are, look. Hundreds of them!" he cried enthusiastically.

Perhaps not quite hundreds, but certainly a lot of minnows. They lay among the stones, facing upstream, their little fins working lazily to keep them stable. As Rob's shadow fell across them they dived out of sight, but soon reappeared. Jimmy waved his jam-jar in front of her nose.

"I've got some big ones to take home."

Rob regarded the half-inch-long captives doubtfully, but decided that discretion would be kinder, and dutifully admired them.

"I see you've got a new hat," she commented.

"Oh, that was Mum. She bought it in Barhill when I lost the old one," he replied disgustedly, dismissing hats as female frailty. Evidently, thought Rob, the thought of what happened to his former battered possession did not bother him.

"Look! There's a big one!"

The child pointed excitedly into the water, and Sam, joining in the fun, thrust his nose in beside the boy's finger. He emerged spluttering, and Jimmy laughed delightedly.

"Sam can't hold his breath under water," he chuckled. "I can—Dad taught me. I can go six strokes before I have to come up for air," he announced proudly.

Rob smiled, remembering his valiant efforts to save himself from the tug of the mill race. His ability to swim had probably saved his life that morning. It had certainly made her own task of rescuing him that much easier, and it explained his calm acceptance of the ducking, afterwards. Laughing, the child patted the water with the flat of his hand, sending a shower of spray over the setter. Red wuffed gruffly, and bounced out of the way, splashing the boy in his turn.

"Hey, stop it, you two!"

Rob gathered her skirts and fled for the footpath, shaking herself free of the myriad drops that clung to her dress. The grass felt warm under her bare feet, and she screwed up her eyes against the green shimmer of it that stretched away towards the hedge without a break, except where a large, dark bulk interrupted the heat-baked stillness of the moribund earth. The dark blob moved, with a different movement from the heat shimmer of the grass, and Rob shielded her eyes with her hand against the glare, to get a clearer look. It still moved, coming in their direction with a purposeful, deliberate progress that all of a sudden stopped the breath in her throat.

"Jimmy!" she whispered.

"Coming, Miss Fenton!" The child splashed across

the water, and scrambled up the bank, waving his jar of minnows gleefully. "Look, I've got a . . . oh!"

Seeing Rob's attention was not on his catch, the boy followed her gaze.

"It's Mr Ford's bull!" His words came in a dry whisper, through a throat constricted by sudden fear. He moved closer to her, his hand going out uncertainly to clutch at her skirts.

"He runs it in a footpath field." The words she had heard at Wade Hollow flashed through Rob's mind, and she was unconscious of speaking them aloud until Jimmy answered her.

"Yes, but never in this one, or Mum wouldn't have let me come here to fish. He's always in the field further downstream, beyond the fence. He must have broken through the hedge."

Remembering the general state of repair at Norton End Farm, Rob did not wonder that the animal had broken through a fence; it would present little difficulty, she thought scathingly. But there was no time for recriminations now. The bull had seen them, and it was obvious that it meant mischief.

"Come here, Red!"

She called the setter to her, speaking quietly, and the dog came with a bound, its game forgotten. Rob blessed the fact that it was well trained, and did not need coaxing to her. She reached out with a hand that trembled, and turned the dog's head towards the approaching animal.

"Over there, Red."

The setter stiffened under her hand, its hackles

rising, communicating the message that it had seen and understood, even before the low snarl musicked through its throat.

"Jimmy." Briefly she hugged the child to her, reassuring him. "Take Sam with you and get on to the other bank, quickly, and run for home."

"There isn't a footpath on that side."

"Never mind about trespassing." Rob understood his objection, but she had to overrule his training now. "Do as I say, there's no time to argue. Run and tell your father. Quickly, now!"

Mention of his father did the trick. Jimmy had every young child's belief that fathers could work miracles, and accustomed to reasonable obedience, the urgency of Rob's command sped his heels homewards. He bundled Sam under his arm and crossed the ford to the other side in one long, continuous watersplash, and with a white-faced backward glance at the tableau across the water he took off at his best speed towards the Martyr's Arms, tossing his fishing net and jam-jar into the play of the stream to free himself for quicker running.

The bull caught sight of the retreating child, and quickened its pace to a trot. It changed course, making for the edge of the ford, and Rob knew with terrible certainty that she must prevent it from reaching the other bank. Jimmy's short legs would not stand a chance against the enraged speed of the huge Friesian cross.

The sight of its quarry disappearing turned the bull's trot into a charge, and in seconds the yards between them became feet. The dog snarled, high-pitched, and Rob glanced down.

"Take him, Red!"

She grabbed her two shoes from the ground at her feet, and ran towards the bull. The dog seemed to understand what she wanted, and flanked out towards the huge beast on its other side. With all the force at her command Rob hurled her shoe at the enormous black face. It struck the bull's forehead and bounced off, and she flung the other. At the same time Red leapt at it from the other side, and the bull pulled up short of the river bank, momentarily confused by the unexpected attack. Red pressed his advantage, snapping at the bull's heels, and emitting a positive volley of high-pitched yelps. The Friesian turned to face its tormentor, but the dog, wary of its horns, kept just out of range, his lithe red body easily twisting out of reach of the great swaying head.

"How like Lewis Ford," thought Rob irrelevantly. "He hasn't even bothered to have the animal de-horned."

Thwarted by the setter's tip-and-run tactics, the bull turned to an easier target. Flicking away the irritation of the constant stream of river gravel that was all Rob could find to throw once she had let her shoes go, the bull spun like a ballet dancer to face her, and with an earth-shattering bellow lowered its head, and charged straight at her. For one paralysing second Rob's legs refused to run. A scream of warning from the dog galvanised her into life again, and she fled at a tangent, away from the line of charge. Once again the bull spun round with incredible speed, and once again it charged.

"How long can this go on?" Rob wondered desperately, gasping under the relentless heat, and yet cold as ice inside her from terror such as she had never known. Her heart thumped agonizingly at the base of her throat until it seemed as if it must choke her.

"Oh, Jimmy, run! Run!" she pleaded silently, knowing that now she had to try to save herself as well as the child.

Three times the bull charged, and three times she managed to evade it by an ever narrowing margin. With something akin to despair, she realised that her strength was running out. Sapped alike by heat and fear, her energy was draining rapidly. The bull paused, and Rob stopped, too, panting, moving backwards slowly, desperate to put space between herself and the maddened animal. It watched her redly, pawing the ground in little eddies of dust, and then suddenly, as if the breathing space had recharged its batteries, it gave another tremendous bellow and hurled itself towards her.

Rob spun round and ran. The few seconds' pause had given her renewed strength, and she exerted all her resources to dodge the murderous charge. For a few seconds she succeeded, her speed taking her across and away from the bull's path, and then her bare foot caught on a sharp, upturned piece of stone, and she slipped. The pain of the raw-edged stone seared through her foot like a hot steel, and she gasped, her leg turning under her. She staggered, hopelessly off balance, and instantly grabbing its advantage, the bull turned on to her, head lowered, intent to kill.

A sharp, unbearable pain seared through her thigh, and she felt herself lifted off her feet. The piled thunder clouds swung in a dizzy arc above her as she hung poised, rag doll-like, over the bull's head. From what seemed to be a long distance away she was conscious of Red's frantic screaming, saw him leap repeatedly at the bull's huge head, and heard, from an even greater distance, the sound of shouts.

With a sharp rending sound, cloth parted from cloth, and the bull's horn disentangled itself at last from her clothing. The animal gave a savage toss of its head, and with a final wild fling they parted company. Rob sailed through the air and hit the ground with a lung-emptying thud. She lay still, helpless now to defend herself, waves of dizziness flooding and receding about her spinning head. From somewhere far above her came the sound of a loud bang.

"The storm has broken at last," she thought hazily. Her one side felt wet. Perhaps it was raining already. The grass was warm and soft, and she turned her face into it gratefully. She knew that she ought to try and get up, try to run away, but she could no longer remember the reason why. Her body felt limp, without sensation, and wearily she let it lie. She tried to think why she had come here, along the river bank. It had something to do with soap, but she was too tired to know what. The storm must be very bad, for it was growing dark. From somewhere miles away on the other side of the darkness, she felt strong arms lift her. Heard a voice whisper close to her ear.

"Rob! Oh, Rob darling. . . ."

And then there was nothing. Nothing but the darkness of the storm.

CHAPTER TWELVE

THE room was strange.

Rob knew that she was not at Mill House, because she could not hear the sound of the mill wheel. And the bed that she lay on had not got the familiar, comfortable dip in the middle. This one was firm and straight. She shifted her position experimentally, and gave a gasp as agony seared through her side. Instantly someone rose from a chair on the other side of the room, and came to her. It was Sue Grant.

"Lie still," she commanded. "You're all bandages."

"No!" Grimly, Rob struggled up on the pillows, and surveyed her surroundings. "Where . . . ?"

"You're at the Martyr's Arms," Jimmy's mother informed her. "Hal carried you here from the ford."

Hallam Rand carried her? So it had not been a dream, she had felt someone's arms about her. But she must have dreamed the voice in her ear. It had called her Rob darling. A rush of memory came to her, and her lips drooped.

Sue Grant, reading the warning signs, and misinterpreting them, got up from the side of the bed.

"Don't move an inch until I bring you a cup of tea."

Rob did not want to. For one thing, she felt stiff all over, and she realised as soon as she tried that she could hardly move her one leg. She must indeed be all bandages, as Sue said. A quick investigation confirmed her hostess's description; her thigh and leg carried as much lagging as a hot water tank in winter, she told herself disgustedly.

She said as much when Sue Grant reappeared with the tray of tea, and Jimmy's mother let out a gurgle of appreciation.

"You sound more like yourself, at any rate."

"What on earth made me go to sleep on your bed?"

"The doctor. You were unconscious when Hal brought you in. The doctor came and patched you up, and gave you a shot to put you out again. And here you are," she finished, handing over a ready stirred cup of tea.

"How long?" It was hot and very sweet, and Rob grimaced but drank obediently, feeling it clear the clouds in her head.

"Since this morning. It's about four o'clock now," she was informed.

Tom Grant popped his head round the door.

"I heard voices?"

"Come on in. I've tried to make her lie down and take things easy, but with that red hair I should have known better," smiled his wife.

"I brought some saddle soap for Jimmy," mourned Rob, remembering clearly enough now. "I dropped it in the field."

"Never mind about the saddle soap," exclaimed Sue. "Fancy thinking of saddle soap at a time like this!"

"Well, we can always find Jimmy some more saddle soap," came a reassuring voice, and Hallam Rand ducked under the door, and stopped at the foot of the bed.

Wearily, Rob closed her eyes. Exhausted and bruised, she did not trust her self-control with Hallam so close to her. She did not see Sue Grant signal to her husband, or hear them leave the room, closing the door gently behind them. She only felt the cup taken from her hand, the side of the bed lift and then go down again, and she opened her eyes to find that the vet had taken Sue's place. She looked away from him, towards the window.

"It's raining," she noticed listlessly.

"Yes, the storm has broken at last."

"I know. It broke while I was in the field. I heard it thunder, and then it went dark."

"The thunder you heard in the field was Bill Wade's gun going off," said the vet softly, his voice gentle, as it was when he talked to Verity. "It's only been raining for the past hour."

"How did Mr Wade come to be in the field?" Rob turned her head to look at him, puzzled. "I sent Jimmy to tell his father," she remembered hazily.

"It's a good job you did," said the vet fervently, his face losing colour at the memory. "The lad came tearing into the Martyr's Arms just as Bill and I decided to drop in for a drink before we went home. We'd been into Barhill together," he explained. "By a wonderful coincidence, Bill had had his gun rebored at the smith's, and he collected it this morning. He stocked up with cartridges while he was there, and brought the lot back with him. If he hadn't been such a crack shot, you might not have been here now."

He swallowed hard, and looked down at her, his face drawn. Rob turned her face back to the window, unable to meet his eyes. Unable to bear his kindness.

"Well, he did, and I am," she said faintly, then paused, hesitating. "Did he—is the bull . . .?"

"Dead. And if Lewis Ford can afford to buy another, he won't be allowed to put it in a footpath field any longer. Bill and I went to the Council House to a meeting this morning, and the alteration to the law on that subject has been officially approved and passed," he said with satisfaction.

"The Council House? But I thought you went to collect the ring?"

The words were out before Rob could stop them. Hallam Rand looked down at her, puzzled.

"The ring? What ring?"

"Verity said she would have her ring today." Rob's whisper was hardly audible.

"So I believe." The vet smiled, and his grey eyes never left her face. "But Martin Bradley wouldn't thank me for collecting the ring for him," he added drily.

"Martin Bradley? But I thought. . . ."

"I don't know what you thought, but I can imagine what Martin and Verity would think if I butted in on their engagement," chuckled the vet, his eyes merry. "By the way, they're keeping their celebration party back for another week until you feel fit enough to go. We can go together," he told her, with evident satisfaction.

Careless of the pain, Rob lifted herself high on her pillows, her eyes bright.

"Here, let me give you a hand."

Gently the vet put his arms about her and lifted her into an easier position. He shuffled himself into a more comfortable position against the head of the bed, and gently pressed her back against him, supporting her against his shoulder. The door opened and Jimmy peeped in, but Hallam did not move, but continued to hold her gently to him, his arms clasped close about her.

"Are you all right?" the child asked breathlessly.

Rob held out her hand to him and smiled, relieved that he seemed none the worse for his recent terrifying experience.

"I'm afraid I lost the saddle soap in the field, Jimmy."

"Oh, that won't matter now, Miss Fenton." Jimmy was philosophical. "Wasn't it marvellous the way Red came to the rescue, Mr Rand? He must be fond of her."

"Yes, Jimmy, very fond of her," smiled the vet, "and so am I. Now that you've seen that Miss Fenton's not at death's door you'd better go and let Sam know, hadn't you?"

The child grinned broadly and disappeared, his footsteps clattering downstairs, and Rob looked up at Hallam Rand, aghast.

"You're very fond of me?"

His arms tightened cautiously about her. "I love you, Rob. I think I have done ever since I pulled you up the bank of the millstream, when you first came to Mill House," he confessed quietly. "I felt so afraid for you that day."

"Oh, Hal!"

Her hands slid along the covers, seeking his. His long, brown fingers found them, curled round them protectively, dark against the white sheet. Rob looked up, and saw in his face the same question that she had seen there before, and had not understood until now. Her lovely, tawny gaze sought his, found and held it until the question in his eyes disappeared, and was replaced by a joyous certainty as she let her head drop back contentedly against his shoulder and relaxed at last, safe in the shelter of his encircling arms.

"After all," he murmured softly, after a pause— a long pause—"if you're going to make a habit of getting into scrapes with young Jimmy, someone will have to be around to bale you out of them. And I seem to have made a habit of it."

Rob stirred and looked up at him again, her eyes

tracing the wavy outline of his dark head against the light bedroom wall.

"You promised me a ride in your Lancia," she reminded him dreamily.

"I know." Hallam smiled down at her, his eyes full of tenderness. "I thought we would use it for our honeymoon."

Have You Missed Any of These Harlequin Romances?

All books are 60c. Please use the handy order coupon.

x

Have You Missed Any of These
Harlequin Romances?

All books are 60c. Please use the handy order coupon.

Y

Have You Missed Any of These
Harlequin Romances?

All books are 60c. Please use the handy order coupon.

Z